Kalamazoo:
Growing Up Sideways in the 1970s

by Winch

ISBN: 0692013865
ISBN-13: 978-0692013861

Library of Congress Control Number: 2011927123

Eight Track Publishing
Milwaukie, Oregon

Versions of these stories appeared in a series of zines.

Special thanks to the readers of those zines, especially the customers at Green Noise Records.

A huge thanks to my family and friends.

Thanks to many of the songsters of Southern Michigan: Holland-Dozier-Holland, Norman Whitfield, Stevie Wonder, Smokey Robinson, Marvin Gaye, Nolan Strong, Hank Ballard, Eddie Floyd, Flo Ballard, Mary Wilson, Wilson Pickett, Andre Williams, Freda Payne, Martha Reeves, Mary Wells, Mack Rice, Barbara Lewis, Aretha Franklin, Jackie Wilson, Del Shannon, Sonny Bono, Jack Nitzsche, Tommy James, Yusef Lateef, Kenny Burrell, John Lee Hooker, Eddie Kirkland, Bryan Gregory, Al Green & the Soul Mates, Earl Van Dyke & the Soul Brothers, Ted Nugent & the Amboy Dukes, Suzi Soul & the Pleasure Seekers, Nikki Corvette & the Convertibles, Brownsville Station, Grand Funk Railroad, The Bob Seger System, The Stooges, The Dogs, Death, Blight, MC5, and the Alice Cooper Group. They taught me how to write stories.

Also thanks to Fred Cole, William Saroyan, and W. C. Fields.

Props to all my students, especially the ones at New Urban High School.

Also props to Tim Thompson and Brian Olson for encouraging my writing, and to all my teachers at Kalamazoo Valley Community College for everything.

And thanks to you, for picking up this book. I hope you like it.

Keep in touch.

winchmartin@live.com

Eight Track Publishing
9408 SE Hollywood Avenue
Milwaukie, OR 97222

eight-track.com

People sometimes think my other stories are true because they're based on junk that really happened, but the truth is most are mostly made up, maybe about 100 proof, half true, half bulldookie, some more like Mad Dog 20/20 with lots of added flavors and coloring to lighten the load on your liver and make them easier to swallow. The stories in this collection are pretty close to the truth, but I still call them fiction because the narrator isn't really me looking back at the days of my youth; that would be boring, and I'd have to tell you what it all means and make some comments about the intolerance and stupidity of the times, warn dimwitted twits not to do the stupid junk in the stories, don't swipe stuff because that's like taking people's work, making them slaves for the hours they spent earning the money to buy that junk, don't joyride because you might get busted, stay in school, say nope to dope and all that, who needs that noise. A voice like that just wouldn't fit the stories so part of the narration is a product of my imagination, more like a kid in Michigan bragging. Sure, maybe the collection begins as an adult looking back, but it's more like a teenager at the end of the decade recalling moments from the previous years, finding former versions of himself as he goes back in time. Since the voices come from younger versions of the author, it may seem silly to call the stories fiction, but I also call them that because it all happened a while ago and I can't recall the exact dialogue or recollect the names of all the players for every story, don't really remember if that was Briggs MacGregor's foxy girlfriend that used to grab my wang in his station wagon, or maybe it was Jake Harley's girlfriend in a Pontiac or something, but this is pretty much the way it went down, not the truth and nothing but, but pretty close, more like moonshine.

For Bob & Dave

PART ONE:
STONERS & BONERS

SIXTEEN
(1979)

It was just me and Dave that summer, the others didn't matter much. They were just Vietnam vets and ex-cons, background noise, like the roar of the chain saws. The boss lived at a halfway house, came to work in an old jean jacket, looked like Lemmy from Motorhead, always wore the same soiled tank top—the kind old geezers wear under their shirts. Every morning, he'd reach into a quarter-pound Ziploc bag and pass out breakfast, white cross and black beauties, RVJ's and RV8's, yellow jackets and pink hearts, a fistful of speed. He'd pour gas in the saws, leave a Kool dangling from his lip. I think his name was Joe.

It was good money, two-fifty an hour, ten-hour days, a pile of machetes and chain saws and all the amphetamines you could eat. Dave was in his element, swinging his sword and shouting like a pirate. Other than that shadow of an Errol Flynn mustache on his lip, he looked to be about twelve years old, strolling down the fallen trees like a kid on the playground playing walk the plank. He'd straddle the mast and hack off the branches. The boss banned him from using the chain saws, wrote him off as an accident waiting to happen. *A fool and his limbs are soon parted. There ain't much you can do about it.*

I couldn't argue with that, but I didn't want to watch that happen. You get attached to your friends so it hurts when one loses a limb. It's almost like losing one of your own. Dave was playing the fool, but he was fun to have around, had something that I was lacking—that spark of innocence still showing in his eyes like the flicker of fireflies in jelly jars. And I didn't have any other friends in that crew. The boss had already warned me about some of them, told me specifics about criminal habits, so I kept my chain saw oiled and ready, tried to prevent the inevitable by keeping an eye on Dave, strapped on my safety goggles and followed behind him, cut the logs after he cleared the branches.

I already knew that my skin was a magnet for flying metal objects, should have known it was only a matter of time before Dave stabbed me with the machete. One morning, it happened. He was in front of me hacking off branches, sliced open my chest with a back

2

swing. I didn't see it coming, and he didn't even notice until I started screaming. Even then he couldn't wipe that shit-eating grin from his face, just looked like a kid that got caught with his hand in some girl's pants. Meanwhile, I was bleeding something fierce so the boss grabbed his Old Grand-Dad from his glovebox and poured a few slugs on my wound, ripped off his tank top and bandaged me up, gave me one of his Kools and we got back to work. We were clearing the land so they could build condominiums. Me and Dave didn't even know what that word meant.

At lunch, we'd shake the sawdust from our mop-tops, tank-top the sweat from our backs. The boss always guzzled a Bud, chucked the empty on the ground. Dave would stomp the can, wrap it around his sneaker, walk around awhile before kicking it loose. It was like he had some rhyme running through his head all the time, some grade-school nonsense that the rest of us had forgotten a long time ago. You couldn't imagine him ever growing up. We'd sit on his car, eat sandwiches on the hood. It was his first ride, a VW wagon, sky blue and rust, bungee cords and duct tape.

When the boss blew the whistle, we'd get back to work. When he blew it again, we'd yell *YUBBA DUBBA DO*. We'd shake off the sawdust and jump in the car. Every day after work, we'd head to North Lake. It was one joint, one beer and one smoke from the job site, if we drove fast enough. We'd hit the Fuzzbuster, use the powerhitter, push an eight-track into the Craig deck, toggle the power-booster, crank *Desolation Boulevard* until the speakers rattled. By the time we chugged the beer and lit the smokes, we were bouncing down the two-track, almost to the lake.

The beach was littered with beer tabs and broken glass, cigarette butts and a dirty diaper. There were never too many people there, just a few old fry-brains with stained jeans and chubby wives, most of them too ancient to climb the rope swing. Dave on the other hand was probably too young, forgot to lift his feet one time. The shallow water by the shore grabbed his ankles, ripped his hands from the rope. When Dave pried his head from the bottom of the lake, he still had that turd-munching grin on his face, his nose broken and bleeding but his eyes still sparkling, his mouth packed with mud. He crawled out of the water and copped a lean against the tree, thought that was just part of the fun. The tree stood a few steps from the water, and farther back was the telephone pole we'd planted in the sand. It was a bit wobbly, but it did the job. We'd nailed a board up high on the pole, across to the tree. We'd tied a rope to a branch.

I'd grab that rope and climb the tree, walk across the board, shimmy up to the tippy-top. Once you balanced your feet on the top of that telephone pole, there was no turning

3

back. You'd flick your smoke and step off, hold tight to the knot as you swung down, lift your feet as you swung up, wait until the rope reached the end of its path. Then you'd let go.

Time slowed down as you sailed through the air. Everything led to that moment when you splashed deep into the water. It was like a cold beer for the whole body. We'd wash the sawdust from our necks, swing on that rope until the cool of night said it's time to go.

Back in the city, we'd hit the party store and cruise the streets, smoke joints and drink beers, crank the tunes and shout at the halter-tops. When Dave would pull up to the curb, I'd bogie my smoke and do my best, give them the only line I knew, *Wanna catch a buzz?* If they leaned over to take a glance, Dave would flash them the high beams. Once they saw that grin, they'd usually hop in. It attracted females like a flashlight attracts fruit flies, maybe reminded them of something, their first wet kisses in the back of the school bus, sharing candy necklaces or catching fireflies in jelly jars, playing spin-the-bottle in sixth grade or playing doctor in the fruit cellar. And it didn't seem to matter to Dave. Nothing could wipe that grin off his face, even if they told us to take a hike.

We'd just park the car and crawl in the caves under the city, flashlights bouncing circles of light against the cement, the rats squeaking and running for cover, the passage getting smaller and smaller as we ran for miles and miles through the innards of the city, the tunnel growing dimmer as the batteries drained. We'd click off the flashlights and use our Zippos to make it back, stop along the way to burn graffiti on the ceiling, cop a lounge in the pitch black, light up a joint. We'd never tell anybody about those caves, never tell ourselves that they were just sewer pipes. We were too busy having a good time.

We did that all summer, working all day, out to the lake every afternoon.

Near the end of August, Dave went up North to see the Cars' *Candy-O* concert with his old friend Rusty. The next time I saw Dave was the last time anybody saw him. I looked down at him, could barely recognize him. Something had wiped that grin from his face. He was dressed in a suit, dead in a coffin. I packed my best bowl, slipped the pipe in his pocket, said *Later on.*

I went back to work for the rest of summer, until school started. We cut down all the trees, chain-sawed them into pieces, fed the branches to the chipper. After we were done, they built the condominiums. Then came the people, the grownups and the kids, boats and mortgages, things we never thought about when we were sixteen.

Dave Middleton
rope swing: 1979

Winch
rope swing: 1979
(photo by Dave)

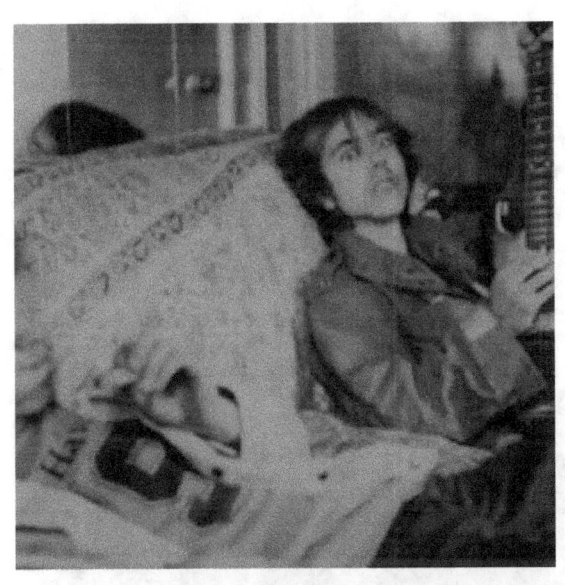

winch
circa 1980
photo by Scott

HUZZY LAKE

Sometimes I'd get sick of the city limits and I'd drive my Olds 98 out to see my cousin Scotty. He wasn't really my cousin, he was my friend Jack's cousin and the Oldsmobile wasn't really mine, it was Jack's, but Scotty's older brother had just died and so had mine, so Jack was my only brother, blood brothers for forever and we both knew life wasn't really worth the hassles, we'd never go to school or get jobs. Sometimes we'd get sick of it all and drive out to Scotty's.

He had a pit in his garage so you could change your oil and drink beers and toke bowls, lolling around with the Ram Jam playing, outside the trees blowing leaves into the garage, so it must have been fall, and when the eight-track paused you could hear Scotty's mom listening to Neil Diamond. That music made me so grim, sadder than Neil Young, all you could do is wait for the click-clank and crank the *Calling Card* by Rory Gallagher, crack open cans of oil and beer, lean over the engine and chuck empties at Scotty in the pit.

The summer before, I'd dropped acid and played horseshoes, and ate hot dogs and went water-skiing and even if Scotty was working at the filling station, we could go smoke dope with Butcher the old Vietnam vet with the wife that Jack knew when he was younger, but Butcher had been a Green Beret, had knives and rifles and he could kill you with his bare hands anyway and besides he was always willing to match a bowl and afterwards we'd hit the lake, crank the *Love It to Death*, drive to the end of the two-track, jump off the cliff. For a moment, all the shit didn't matter, and the water was cool, like a Popsicle on a stick to some shirtless kid standing on the sidewalk with a stubbed toe.

But summer was over and fall came like I already told you, eating acid all the time, hanging lazy in the city, swiping cigarettes by the carton, eight-tracks by the dozen at the indoor shopping mall, *Heavy Petting* and *Bad Reputation*, *Highway to Hell* and *Hell Bent For Leather*, out in the cemetery with the car doors open, the Sex Pistols cranking, sleeping against tombstones, waking cold in my army jacket with leaves in the collar, Jack freezing in his sleep with his hair cut crazy, no sleeves on his black T-shirt, beer bottles by his head, and then came winter and fishtailing out of town out to Huzzy Lake

9

when the snow was deep as a ditch and we'd roar out of the forest on a Ski-Doo snowmobile, me on the back and holding on tight as we busted out of the shadows and out on the lake and I thought the ice might crack and we'd drown in the icy water, drop down to the clay-cold mud of Huzzy Lake. The idea seemed as sad as growing old and listening to Neil Diamond. But of course the ice held up and when you'd step off the snowmobile, the ground gave a few inches like dirt over a fresh grave, but there was a shack for ice-fishing, beers in the snow, songs on the transistor radio, the crisp air spiked with something that almost seemed like hope.

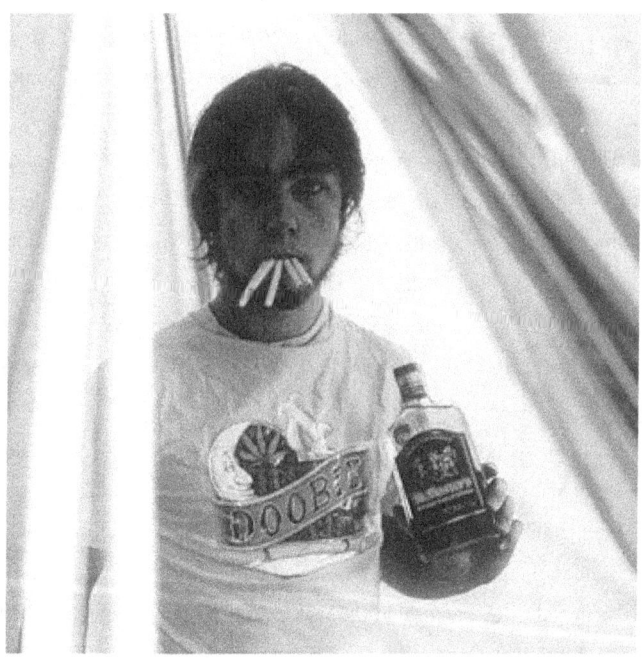

Winch
circa 1981

Tani's first attempt on the rope swing. Unfortunately, she didn't understand the importance of letting go. After this, she just watched.

Jack and Margo

Me and Jack

Winch
circa 1973

YES, THERE REALLY IS A KALAMAZOO

Kalamazoo is a real place, where I grew up. It's in Michigan, about halfway between Detroit and Chicago, the home of Wings Stadium and the State Hospital, the insane asylum on top of the hill, crazy people all over town, the city where they made Gibson guitars and Checker cabs, more Oldsmobiles and Chevys than anybody can count. We had colleges too, WMU and K. College, about a zillion people working at Fisher Body, the GM plant where they made the car bodies, shipped them over to Detroit for the frames and power plants. All those factories are closed up now, but I'm not talking about now. I'm talking about the past, the days of my youth.

Back then, our neighborhood was jam-packed with cars and kids, winter-beaters by the curb, rust-buckets in the driveways, half-built muscle cars in the garages, mostly GM, Ford and Mopar, a few AMCs and imports, kids everywhere, some running through the sprinklers, others hop-scotching and pedaling Stingrays in the streets, skateboard-riding down the sidewalks, most swarming the mobile pool when it came. If the baby-boom were a train, we would have been the overloaded caboose.

Of course, I don't really think of us as part of the boom, can't relate with those folks, didn't know where I was when any of the Kennedys got shot, didn't even know Woodstock happened. It was *Happy Days* and *The Brady Bunch*, Evel Knievel and Muhammad Ali, Mario Andretti and Richard Petty, O. J. Simpson and Joe Namath, Mark Spitz and Jean-Claude Killy, Wilt Chamberlain and Kareem Abdul-Jabbar, Bobby Orr and Burt Reynolds, Alice Cooper and Grand Funk Railroad, the Jackson Five and hard rock and not much else.

Large families were normal as having three or four four-door sedans in the driveway back then but ours still stood out like a rust-bucket in a nice neighborhood. "How many you got in your family, Winch?"

"I dunno." There was a bunch of us. "Quit axin' me that."

We were the oddball family of the neighborhood, the Winch clan, we got blamed for everything, did most of it. My dad had a bearskin coat, a beard and hair like Jeremiah Johnson, ax and hand saw, our front yard was wood. My bedroom was a long ways from the fireplace so it was cold all winter. "Shoot Winch, you can see your breath in your room."

"Big deal." Dad was great, a full-fledged cheapskate, took the garbage to work to save money, put a brick in the toilet to conserve water, stuffed our pockets with stove-popped popcorn when we went to the movies. Once a year, we'd go out to eat.

"Sir, would you like to test drive something today?"

"No, we're just here for the hot dogs."

"And Coke," I added. It was the only time I got pop. I lived on Wyler's and Tang, Space Sticks and Funny Face, Jolly Olly Orange and Lefty Lemon-Lime, Quaker and Quisp and King Vitamin, had to mix powdered milk with the real stuff, had to greaze fast or go hungry, had to get up early if you wanted the prize in the cereal box.

Going to a fancy restaurant was another story, only happened after a trip to the emergency room. Of course, getting hurt came to me naturally, just like falling down. It was a cinch to get an injury, just meant breaking a bone or eating some poison, or doing something so I needed stitches. If I did that, Mom would take me to Burger Chef on the way home from Bronson Hospital. I went there a lot, ate mothballs and chugged turpentine, found shotgun shells and whacked them with a hammer. When my brother Doug stuck a bobby pin in the outlet, the lights went out, his arm exploded, busted open, smoke coming out the gashes up his arm. That was cool. I bet he got a burger and fries for that.

Baby-sitters around the neighborhood had learned that the money earned wasn't worth the hassles, wasn't worth the scars and bruises, a few greenbacks didn't pay for the hospital bills and years of therapy that came after watching the Winch clan for a few nights, learned that lesson the hard way, spread the word like a tornado warning. Of course, that was all part of our battle strategy, proof that the propaganda campaign was working. Most baby-sitters were two-faced teenyboppers, jawing on the telephone and raiding the cupboards as soon as our parents split. And they were bitter because the Winch cupboards didn't have much of value. They were just wasting their time and wasting our parents' money. We weren't babies and didn't need some pimple-faced brat telling us what to do. We were more than prepared to take care of ourselves. We took action.

We'd look in the mirror and practice our evil glares, compare our stink-eyes, roll our eyeballs and fold our eyelids, foul up our faces with dirt and pretend we were a clan of devil-children. We had no problem playing the part, were full of snakes and snails, had snail-trails smeared across our sleeves, snake skins in cigar boxes, had gone from clean-cut buzz cuts to messy mop-tops long before that was normal for most kids. We were naturally rowdy, brave as soldiers. We were prepared for battle. "Red Beard used to catch his beard on fire before he'd launch an attack."

"That's heavy duty."

"You think w'oughta do that too?"

"We don't got no beards."

"That's true." My own weapons of choice were SSP racers, the Siamese Slingshot and the Bush Burner, Richard Petty's Plymouth Superbird, each one of them a mass of metal and plastic, a speeding bullet with a poisoned letter. The Superbird could take the spike from a high-heeled shoe.

Once you had the target on the ground or without shoes, you could finish her off. If she came with low-top sneakers, it was the same as bare feet. It was time for the Bush Burner.

She'd be leaning against the counter, yapping on the yellow wall phone, twirling the cord around her finger. I'd yank the ripcord, listen to the supersonic sound, put the spinning wheel to the ground. The car would jump from my hand, howl across the wood floor, slam into the exposed ankle. If she thought that was just by accident, I'd sit up on my scabby knees and let my arms dangle, drag my knuckles across the floor, cock my head and glare at her through my eyebrows. I'd pretend to be a devil-child. If she didn't get that hint, the message became clear when she'd read the bloodstained letter attached to the car. *You are ugly and stupid. I hate your guts. This is our house and you don't belong here. If you value your life, don't come back.*

Even when my folks upped the ante, nobody seemed to be home, or at least they wouldn't come to the phone. "How come we have such troubles finding a baby-sitter?"

"Don't look at me." She couldn't blame just me. "I didn't do it."

"Didn't do what?"

"We can take care of ourselves."

"We'll see about that."

"Okay." The first time my parents left us alone, we tied my sister Janet to the pipes under the bathroom sink, so we could see our TV show without her nagging about watching *The Red Balloon* again, Kukla, Fran and Ollie. My dad was ticked when he got home, got out the wooden spoon. Sure it hurt, but we had no regrets. We'd watched *Mighty Mouse* that morning, as it should be.

16

After a while, my parents realized they still needed to find some peace of mind, had their own wounds that needed healing, finally gave in to our demands. They figured they'd give us another chance, left us alone in the evening, left behind a pan of goulash for us to share for dinner.

Of course, my big brother Mike had gotten tired of sharing, sick of splitting the grub with all the endless hatchlings of a Catholic family, each and every one of them with a pair of meat-hooks at the ends of his or her arms. Mike figured he'd go back to the good old days, eliminate some of the competition, shoved me and my little brothers in the closet, didn't know why I was yelling, didn't realize he'd slammed my hand in the hinge. He got a chair to reinforce the door, grabbed the pan of dinner, came back and sat on the chair, started in on the goulash. Finally Kenny told him what had happened, why I was yelling. It wasn't just because he'd locked me in the closet, it was more than that and Mike finally understood that. He opened the door and flipped out, felt really rotten when he saw what he'd done to my flesh and bones, offered me some dinner, but I was too busy trying to put my hand back together, spurting blood all over, so he wrapped up my wounds with a shirt and fed me a bunch of the painkillers he'd gotten from one of his accidents. "We gotta get you to the hospital."

"How we gonna get there?" It's hard to thumb a ride without a thumb.

"I'll get the neighbors." We made it to Bronson Hospital, but the dimwitted lady at the counter wouldn't help me. She needed a permission slip from my parents or something.

"We have to wait for your mother. Grab a seat."

"WHAT?" I can't grab a seat. "My hand hurts."

"Just be patient."

"I am a patient. This is the emergency room, ain't it?"

"We can't do anything until your mother arrives."

"WHAT?" That didn't seem right to me so I unwrapped my hand and showed her my emergency, spurted blood all over her dress. "Don't that look like an emergency to you?"

"We better get you admitted."

"I'm glad you admit that." So they let me into the room and sewed my thumb back on. While they were doing that, my mom showed up, took me to Burger King, told my brother he could have the leftover goulash when we got home, got me the crown for my head and a Whopper burger for my belly. They say you need two hands to handle that, but I did all right with just one.

"Is it good?"

"It's humungous." It was my first Whopper. "And it tastes terrific."

"Mike feels really bad."

"He didn't mean to do that."

"Did those pills he gave you help?"

"I think." I think I was wasted.

"Maybe I should buy him a burger when he comes back from the bathroom."

"Yeah." I wasn't mad about him hurting my hand, that was just by accident. I was just mad about him cheating me out of the goulash.

"Why did he put you boys in the closet?"

"Beats me." The plan was to help him get my brothers in the closet, and then he was supposed to let me out and we'd split the dinner. But he never planned to share that, just knew it'd be easier to get all of us in there with my help. "We were just playin' a game."

"I hope you all learned your lesson."

"Yeah." Mike got too greedy with the goulash. He got that but didn't get a chance to eat it. He'd get a burger but that would look pretty dinky next to my Whopper. "I think we learned that."

After I got the stitches out, I went over to Harley's house. His parents were gone and my hand was getting better so me and him had a sword fight with butcher knives. Of course, he had the upper hand, could use one hand to hold the lid of a pan to block my attack. I had to use my arm.

So he won the battle, cut open the sleeve of my jean jacket, sliced my elbow down to the bone. But it didn't really hurt and looked pretty trick with the bone sticking out, blood running down my arm and dripping on the yellow kitchen linoleum. I didn't even know he got me until I saw that.

"You're bleedin' bad." Harley felt really rank when he saw all that blood, tried to give me one of his brother's records, one by Slowhand Eric Clapton. "Take it."

"I don't want it." I didn't even have a record player. I had an eight-track deck, and now I had a cool bloodstained rip on my jean jacket. I figured we'd call it even. "I hate that album."

"What about this?"

"Awright." It was *E. Pluribus Funk* by Grand Funk Railroad. I grabbed that and hoofed on home. But the gash wouldn't stop bleeding so I had to go to the hospital, had to fib to the doctor, tell him that I fell on glass. "I was hoofin' home from Harley's, slipped on Henderson Drive." The doctor knew it was a knife wound, thought I was in a rumble or something, called the fuzz.

Of course I didn't tattle. You never rat out your friends, not in my neighborhood. I stuck to my story, got some stitches. I got a good scar. I've still got it.

Harley had more wounds than the rest of us combined. He was just what you call accident prone. It was a problem he had. One time, his brother Jake chucked him out the front window, and another time I was walking home from Cub Scouts, ran into him. "What's the deal?"

"I got hit by a car."

"Shoot." He didn't look so good. "Y'awright?"

"I dunno." He turned around to show me his back. "My shoulder's killin' me."

"I bet." It was a compound fracture, collarbone sticking out. The guy hit him and took off, hit and run. I helped him home, didn't even tease him when he started crying.

Later, Harley would get other scars, and so would I, even two big holes in my skull, but I'll tell you about that later. Right now, I'm trying to stick with the elementary-school years. In those days, there were two kinds of kids, ones that stayed home and did whatever, and the others that went to the park for a game of smear-the-queer, the Harleys and Pulaskis, Steve and Mark, tons of others, older kids like Briggs MacGregor, sometimes Mediocre Crocker or the Lewis boys.

If you haven't played smear-the-queer, it's simple as spitting goobers, like football without so many rules, you just chuck the pigskin in the air, someone picks it up and runs. The one with the ball is a one-man team, everyone else on the defense. We'd chase him down, smear the queer. He'd wipe the blood from his face and chuck the ball in the air. Someone else grabs it. If someone broke something, or needed stitches, one of us would walk him home. The rest would keep playing, until the dinner bells rang. After supper we'd play some more, until the sun went down.

Sometimes at night we'd play ding-dong ditch 'em, ring the bells and book. Usually we'd just play ditch 'em, a game that combined hide-and-seek and tag. If you were it, you'd count to a hundred, scream *READY OR NOT*. If you were found, you'd run away. If you got tagged, you'd help get the others. If you couldn't find them, you'd scream *ALLY-ALLY OXEN FREE*.

We played that game most every night, a million times, with the girls and everyone, there wasn't much else to do, just *Gilligan's Island* after school, swimming in the traveling pool in the summer, playing trampoline on the pole-vault mat at Angel Field, skeeching and Snurfing in the wintertime.

During most of the games, I racked up scars to remember them. Parts of my body are like pages in a diary, entries written with a permanent marker.

STINGRAYS & STATION WAGONS

In the winter, you had skeeching and Snurfing, sword fighting with icicles and tunneling through the snow, building igloos and bombing cars with snowballs, stretching the hose from Harley's yard to Henderson Park, hosing down the basketball court and waiting for it to freeze, playing ice hockey as soon as it did. When Briggs MacGregor tooled down Henderson Drive with his first set of wheels, we were on it like rats on a dropped sandwich. We rode that station wagon like a surfboard, butted one sneaker against the hood ornament, leaned back with one palm on the hood to keep from falling. He'd click on his seat belt and peel out through the ice, race down the alley and slam head on into a snowbank. You'd go flying, sailing for days, get up and wait for your next turn.

Briggs's foxy girlfriend would always ride shotgun, sporting her big glasses that changed to shades in the sunlight. Briggs wouldn't want us in the car, but she'd talk him into it, let us all in the front seat, let me sit right on her lap. She'd always put her hand right on my ding-dong, give my thing a squeeze. I always wondered if that was just by accident, but now I know it wasn't. I'd grab the dashboard, bite my bottom lip and try not to lose it, elbow Harley in the seat next to me, nod my chin and he'd look down. We wouldn't say a thing, but later we'd bust our guts and slap our knees, laugh about that for hours. She was a naughty girl, but I didn't mind it. When the ice melted, there was still plenty of fun to be had. You'd grab it with both hands and hold on tight.

When Briggs came around, we'd all go native on him, attack his station wagon like a bunch of spear-chuckers hunting a rhino, jump on it without him stopping, the lucky ones on the roof with the luggage rack, me and Harley grabbing where the hood meets the wipers, holding on for our lives and hoping for the best, bellies sliding across the metal when he'd whip around the corners.

"HOLD ON FOR YOUR LIFE."

"I'M TRYIN'."

"KEEP DOIN' THAT." I couldn't let go to help him. "DON'T GIVE UP."

"I'M A GONER."

"NO YOU AIN'T."

"It's been nice knowin' you."

"There's a stop sign comin' up."

"I CAN'T MAKE IT."

"You can do it."

"I'M SLIPPIN'."

"He's slowin' down."

"I'M JUMPIN' OFF."

"Same here." That's what you call being scared of something. That was the first time I felt that feeling. "THAT WAS SOMETHIN' ELSE."

"And then some." Harley fell down on the grass. "I can't believe I'm still alive."

"I KNOW." I'd just learned that you didn't need to hot-box cigars or pop pills to catch a buzz. You've got free buzz materials right inside you, just got to know how to tap them. I felt like I'd just got born. I scoped out the wicked curve that whipped around Treeless Park, and the dirt road to Angel Field. It was like seeing it all for the first time. "I was scared almost to death."

"I think I pissed in my pants."

"I CRAPPED A BIG-FAT TURD IN MINE. I almost did that."

"That was a trip and a half."

"That's what you call THE ULTIMATE." That's what I call it. "It was a blast."

"For days."

"Just think about this. When we get old, we can do that all the time."

"Every day of the week."

"I'm hip." And twice on Sunday. "I can't wait."

Before we could get our own cars, we had to start with skateboards and Stingrays. I'll save the skateboard stories for later, wait until the urethane wheels arrive from California, introduce you to Louie and the fun we had once that happened. In the meantime, I had my secondhand Stingray, not a cable on the whole contraption, coaster brakes and nothing but, one speed and one speed only, gunpowder blue with white pinstripes, banana seat patched with Wacky Pack stickers.

I'd ride that two-wheeler all the time, cut the clothesline and square-knot it to the sissy-bar. On the other end, I'd noose a hangman's knot around the neck of my sister's Barbie. I'd drag that doll until her head popped off, ride that bike until the sun went down.

One day, the private-school Richie-Rich kid got a brand-new Huffy Thunder Road. It had a stick shifter on the bar, three speeds, two too many. We sent that bike on a ghost-ride down Suicide Hill, held that brat against the fence, made him watch. When we let him go, he ran home crying. That was great, made me feel like I'd done something worthwhile with the afternoon.

Suicide Hill was actually Burrows Road, ran along the sledding hill at Angel Field. That street was steep, the pavement all tore up, finally leveled out when it hit the big sign shaped like a cowboy hat, Arby's Roast Beef Sandwiches, that restaurant had just been invented. And that road made for a good dare. You'd try to ride the slope without slowing down, keep your legs out to prove you weren't hitting the brakes, dive-bomb down the hill and hope for the best.

I don't think anybody ever made it. You either wimped out or wiped out. But you'd reward yourself anyway, go to Arby's and rogue some greaze, tell that pimple girl at the register to slice us up some sandwiches. No we ain't got no money, but we've got a pocket of punch cards we stole from you yesterday, so get going, stoner girl. Once this lady found my older brother Bob knocked out on the side of that hill. He got a concussion, didn't remember what happened. We knew.

Even my little brother Kenny tried to conquer that hill. It nearly ruined his future family life. When I came home that day, he was spread-eagled in the hallway. "What's the deal?"

"Nothin'." I guess he didn't want to talk about it.

"What's wrong with Kenny?" I asked my dad.

"Leave him alone."

"What happened?"

"He wiped out on his bicycle. On Burrows Road."

"Is he okay?"

"I'll put it this way. His scrotum sack is big as a cantaloupe."

"Oh." Ouch.

GO CARTS & MINI BIKES

When we got older, we needed more speed, built go-carts, Briggs and Strattons on sheets of plywood, two axles, no brakes. We'd race around the graveyard like Mario Andretti, ripping around the curves, sliding across the gravel. It was tons of fun. One time I crashed into a tombstone, lost a few teeth, put them under my pillow, scored a few quarters. I had no regrets.

Caveman showed up at the playground one day with a brand-new store-bought mini-bike. "Check out what I got for my birthday."

"Killer. Can I ride it?"

"No way."

"Yeah right."

"I can't. My mom said. N-O spells nope. Nobody can ride it."

"That's not what your mom said to me last night. When I had my thing in her thing. I humped her poontang, rode her like a mini-bike all night." I yanked the handlebars from his hands. "Give it."

"Be careful with it."

"I will." I started it up, skanted around the playground, headed toward the baseball game. I was no good at that game, needed eyeglasses but refused to wear them, always struck out when I went to the plate, decided not to play anymore. But that day I figured I'd get my revenge.

I hit second base at top speed, sent everyone running for cover, rounded third, headed for home. I bent back full throttle, leaned over as I slid across the plate. I bailed just before the bike crashed into the backstop. My right leg hit the pole.

"YOU BROKE MY MINI-BIKE!"

"Yep." It was busted in two, only the cables holding the forks to the rest of the bike. "It was brand-new."

"So what?" I couldn't stand up, slapped the dust from my cords. "Big deal."

"Y'awright?" Pulaski asked me.

"Yeah." I pulled up the cuff of my bell-bottoms. "No blood."

"I saw some. It's soakin' through your cords. Pull up your pant-leg again."

"Awright." So I did, this time a little farther.

"SEE, I TOLD YOU."

"Yep." Pulaski was right. The skin was split to bone, my shin sticking out. It was numb so it didn't hurt yet. It was neat to see. Bones hold you up all your life so it's always cool to see one.

"You better not tattle, Caveman. Winch got hurt. He's hurt bad. Really bad."

"I won't."

"He could sue you."

"He could?"

"Yeah. For about a million dollars."

"Y'aint gonna, are you?"

"Not if you don't narc."

"I won't." Caveman held up the handlebars, looked at the rest on the ground. "I'll say I broke it. By accident."

"Good." Good deal.

"You awright?"

"Yeah." I got a killer scar, permanent for sure. Everything worked out.

BLACK CATS & CHERRY BOMBS

The other cool junk about summer was the Fourth of July, firecrackers to be exact, all kinds and colors. We'd let them off in our hands, start with Ladyfingers to toughen our fingertips, move on to Zebras and Black Cats, if you felt like being a bad-ass. I always felt like that, had gunpowder stains on my fingers, ringing in my ears. "I'm a bad-ass."

"What?" Harley had hearing problems, for some reason. "What's the deal?"

"You deaf or somethin'?"

"Just in this ear. You know that."

"I said, I'm a BAD-ASS."

"More like a DUMB-ASS."

"Same difference." When the tulips opened, we'd drop Black Cats into the blooms, line them up and light them off. We'd blow those flowers to smithereens, make an explosion of mass psychedelic proportions, leave nothing but a row of green stems. That was the best.

One time we got M-80's and cherry bombs, from this kid leaning against his Pontiac. He popped the trunk, had it filled with fireworks, lit the fuses with the end of his Lucky Strike, gave us a show so we could decide which ones to get. We got the big ones, grabbed them with both hands.

"You don't want those to go off in your hand."

"How come?"

"They'll take your fingers. Half of your scrawny arm with 'em."

"Cool." The Richie-Rich kid had just gotten a new Tonka truck, was showing it off at Henderson Park. "I bet a firecracker wouldn't even hurt that."

"Nothing can hurt this."

"Uh-huh." We set that dump truck in the middle of the sandbox, put a cherry bomb between the wheels. I lit the stick match on the zipper of my cut-offs. "STAND BACK."

"It won't hurt it."

"We'll see." I cupped the match and put the flame to the fuse, listened to it sizzle down and stepped back to watch the show. We held our breaths and covered our ears.

"It's a dud."

"Just wait." The bomb exploded like a nuclear blast, lifted that truck on a four-foot mushroom cloud. The toy hung there for a moment, pieces flying everywhere. A wheel came whizzing at me, flying too fast for me to duck. It caught me under the eye, sliced the skin wide open, down to the cheekbone. We split that scene like bandits, left that kid with his mouth wide open, jumped on our Stingrays and pedaled away, laughing to ourselves and hollering out loud, my eye swelling shut, blood spraying across my cheek, a greasy smile smeared across my face. "THAT WAS KICK."

"AND KILLER."

"I'm hip." That's a fact.

"Slow down a sec."

"How come?"

"What happened to your face?"

"Got hit with shrapnel."

"It don't look good."

"Who cares." With bottle-rockets and Roman candles, we'd split into teams, have battles in the streets, World War III every day of the week, use the metal lids from garbage cans for shields. We'd chuck smoke bombs in open windows, ticking people off, having fun. "LET'S BOOK."

"BUT NOW." With snakes, we'd head over to the college, sit in the lobby and grind up a couple dozen in the bottom of an ashtray, mix them up with the sand, wait and watch. When someone would sit down and snuff out a smoke, the tray would explode with snakes, hundreds of them sizzling out of the black smoke. That would flip people out. It was kick, blowing up junk and having a blast. We stretched that fun like a glob of Bazooka, all the way to the end of summer.

"What's next?"

"WHATEVER." After we killed off the fireworks, we'd get the vampire blood at Tiffany's Party Store, go down to the nameless park by West Main Hill, stand by the side of the four-lane and play Big Time Wrestling, pour the blood over our faces and beat the crap out of each other, wait until people pulled up to stop us. We'd give them the sign, tell them to bite the big one, run off laughing our heads off. It was great, busting Jack-O-lanterns on Halloween, siphoning gas and burning junk, smearing big jars of rubber cement across the street, lighting the smear on fire, hiding in the bushes and waiting for the cars. Usually they'd back up, but once in a while, some bad-ass would drive through

27

the wall of flames, probably thinking it was gasoline, the glue sticking to the whitewalls, the flames spinning around like pinwheels. It was like the Fourth of July in October.

URBAN ANIMALS

Wildlife was nearly extinct in our neighborhood, mostly just us and the rats down by the creek, possum eyes glowing in the sewer at night. Pollution wiped out most anything born from an egg, and without a lot of birds, the bugs were bad, mosquitos the worst. Shoe flies didn't bother me, but those mosquitos got on my nerves. But I'd get them back.

When those buggers would try to tap my arm, I'd pull the skin taut, trap their stingers until they sucked out the stuff that made your skin itch, until their bellies swelled like little water balloons under the faucet. They just didn't know how to stop themselves from sucking. You could almost hear them screaming. It was kick, something good to make from the rotten.

We had lightning bugs too, thousands of fireflies lighting up the sky at night. We'd whack them with badminton rackets, with anything you had, drop them into jelly jars till you had yourself a lantern. When we had a good catch, we'd smash them to smithereens, smear the bug guts over our faces, in our hair, all down our arms. We were like lords of the fireflies, glowing in the dark.

And we had tons of bats swooping out of the darkness when we'd chuck gravel in the air. They thought the rocks were bugs. I could do that for hours.

During the day, we had some squirrels up in the trees, other ones yapping from the telephone wires, running across the grass. One day, I decided to try and get one. "See that squirrel?"

"Yep." It was a good twenty feet away.

"Check this out." I took out my Old Timer, flicked open the blade.

"You can't hit that."

"I can try." Evel Knievel could jump over a box of rattlesnakes, maybe I could do this. I'd gotten pretty good at chucking knives, used my dart board for practice.

"I dare ya."

"Awright." I held the blade, flung it at the squirrel, couldn't believe it when it stuck. The squirrel screeched, shook it loose, hightailed up the telephone pole.

"Dang. You did it, Winch."

"Yep." I felt bad for that squirrel, but he seemed okay. And my friends were pretty impressed, patted me on the back. I was like Ted Nugent that day.

GOING UNDERGROUND

When I was real little, there were crayfish and salamanders crawling in the sewer creek by the tracks. Me and my brothers used to catch them and put them in Dixie cups, sell them around the neighborhood. A cheap pet, a critter in a cup. The going price was two bits, a pretty good deal for everyone involved, especially us. It was just one branch of Winch Industries, like the Hot Wheel Winternationals in the basement, collecting a nickel for every entry. Sometimes that meant serious money if a kid brought his whole collection of cars, especially if he hadn't learned his multiplication. Like they say, a dimwit and his dimes are soon divided.

We'd set up the orange track the night before, tack the starting gate to the basement stairs, slide the pieces together, install the automatic checkered-flag gizmo by the fruit cellar, flatten some boxes and bust out the markers, draw boxes for all the cars, dinky rectangles that made a huge triangle. We had two friends that would help out with construction, muscleman Mike Olexia and whiz-kid Andrew Smith, both of them doing their parts to make it run smoothly. The contestants would show up after Saturday morning cartoons, pay their fees and line up their roadsters on that piece of cardboard. Each row led to the next until it came down to the final round. We'd take a lunch break before we'd launch that, give the winner a ribbon and a pat on the back, pocket the earnings.

When the snow melted, we had the backyard Kool-Aid Karnival, games of chance and an obstacle course, refreshments on the midway. I covered the snack bar and ran the adding machine, counted up the earnings, sold salamanders on the side. But by the time I was in elementary, we had to limit the business to the basement tournaments and backyard carnivals because the ecology was going downhill, pollution had killed the animals off, ruined our days of selling dirt-cheap pets.

I knew about that ecology, had that green patch on my jean jacket, knew all about pollution too, had watched *Godzilla and the Smog Monster*, felt bad for that Indian on that public announcement by the Ad Council, that's a crying shame, people start pollution, people can stop it, so I decided to give a hoot and not pollute, but I couldn't see any reason to not be a litterbug at the sewer creek. It was beyond hope, but we didn't mind, made the best of it. On the weekend, me and my brother Bob would walk by there on the way to catechism. We'd find banana-split boats, float them down the waterway, have races, chuck rocks and dirt-bombs when the boats got caught up. We'd follow the race as long as it went, all the way to where the only white kids were me and my brother.

At one point, the creek went underground but that didn't stop us. There was a tiny ledge on the wall that you could shuffle across, if you were a real bad-ass. I wanted to be that, so I decided to try it. My brother had already done it so it was my turn.

It was pitch dark under the road, just the rumble of cars above, the sewer sluicing below, and squeaking sounds, something crawling over my sneakers. I had seen *Willard* and *Ben* at the double-feature drive-in show, knew what those rats could do if a bunch of them got mad at you, so I let them be, but when one started crawling up my tube sock, I had to kick it loose. It splashed in the water below. The other ones started squealing to each other and I was hoping they wouldn't get too ticked off, would realize I had to do that. I was pleading with them and praying to God, saying I'd stop picking on my brothers and stealing Pepsi pop from the church and all that bad junk if I could just make it out of that tunnel before the rats got me. I was pretty scared, I admit that.

But the army of rats decided not to eat me alive and finally I made it around the corner, could see the light at the end of the tunnel. I was feeling pretty good, when I got out of there. The sun looked brighter than I'd ever seen it. It was scary doing that and it gave my nightmares, but if you want to be a bad-ass, you have to do junk like that. It was something to do. It was fun. That's what it was.

Before we headed home, we had a foot race on the railroad tracks, side by side, like walking the tightrope. If you fell off, you had to do a five-apple count before you'd start again. He won of course but it didn't matter, he was supposed to win because he was older. And I didn't care because we'd both made it through the tunnel. We were like brothers. In fact, that's what we were.

"What happened?" my mom asked me when we got home. "How come you're so filthy?"

"Just 'cause." They were just hand-me-downs, like all my clothes. "'Cause I am."

"Oh," she said. She wasn't one of those moms that asked too many questions, or that got mad about getting filthy-dirty. She hardly got mad about anything. "How was catechism today?"

"Good," my brother told her.

"Yeah," I said. "Pretty good." Me and my brother grinned at each other. Then we sat down at the table for a boloney and butter sandwich, crunched up some Be-Mo's to add some texture, potato chips so fresh they were sometimes still warm in the bag, even had an honest slogan, *more vigor and less figger*. We had ourselves a good lunch. I felt like I'd earned it.

SNURFING

My brother Bob taught me to skeech, taught me good, I was really good at it, probably the best in the whole wide world. I did a lot of that in the elementary years, but when I think of skeeching, I think of Louie Palladino, and I didn't meet him until junior high, so those stories will have to wait.

In elementary, winter mostly meant grabbing the Snurfer.

Snurfing was an early version of snowboarding, surfing the snow, s-n from snow, the rest from surfing, there you had it. It all started in Michigan, water-skiing down the sand dunes at Lake Michigan, in the winter when the snow was deep. Brunswick had the wood shop, took the idea and went with it, started making Snurfers. They looked just like a water-ski, with a rope knotted to the front, something to hold. The first models were the best, made of wood, painted brown, had steel rudders on the bottoms. Santa asked what I wanted, and me and my brothers all wanted Snurfers. We got them too, under the tree. We ripped off the ribbons and hit the hills.

Of course, we had sleds made of wood and metal, and plastic saucers, and inner tubes. And the family toboggan. We'd stand on that, way at back, hold the rope, ride it like a long board. But Snurfers went with Winch like sugar goes on cereal. We all got one, rode them all winter.

My brother Bob was the king of the board, but I was pretty good, had tons of places to ride, Castle Hill right by my house, K. College practically in my backyard. At the college, you didn't even need to bring a board. They'd leave out the fiberglass lunch trays for anyone to use. And you could ride them deep into the evening because they had lamps and flood lights that lit up the hill at night. Those lights made my day, shining on the slopes like candles on my birthday cake.

And the icing on the cake was all the college girls. They were spread across that campus like they were going out of style, sporting yellow parkas and burnt-orange skiing vests, shiny leggings and moon boots and ear muffs, running out after supper to ride the trays with us, playing smash-up derby and spinning down the hill, jumping on the toboggan and we'd ride it together, leaning back with our arms and legs wrapped around each other. After a while, they'd get tired and wipe the snow from their soggy butts, need to take a break for a smoke. They rolled their own, got all jolly and shiny-eyed afterwards. We'd keep riding while they went to get the munchies and hot cocoa.

When they came back, they'd let me push my cold fists into their warm muffs, those furry tunnels that college girls had back then, fuzzy on the outside, silky and snug on the inside. They'd give me a sip and I'd watch them wipe the foam from their mouths. For some reason, I could watch them drink cocoa all night, just had this thing for college girls. And that thing was growing.

"Do you have to go to the bathroom?"

"No." I just got really excited looking at those girls. And they got really excited when I'd whip out the Snurfer. They'd sit on the stairs and sip on their hot chocolates, slide their hands in their muffs and watch me do my stuff. They said they'd never seen anything like it. I'd mount the board and slide it back and forth to break the ice and heat up the wax, put on my race face and bring the nose to the edge of the slope, tease them a bit, bring their soggy butts to the edges of their seats. No bookworm boyfriend could compete with me and my Snurfer. I knew that for a fact.

My Snurfer cut through the snow like putting a greased boner to an oversized albino girl. I'd drop down the face and over the moguls, into the groove and over the sidewalk, cap the show with an explosion through the snow-covered brush by the foot of the hill. The girls would clap for me and I'd get up and do it again. I could do that all night when I was young. It was a blast.

Snurfers had rubber knobs to keep your sneakers from sliding but nothing to keep you from flying when you wiped out. It was almost more like surfing than snowboarding, like skateboard-riding on the snow. One time Harley was going down Castle Hill, ran into the bushes at the bottom, went sailing through the air, over the bush. You were supposed to bust through the brush, but he made the mistake of hitting the trunk. It was just by accident so without even trying, he invented some brand-new amusement. That invention became a wintertime tradition.

Near the bottom of the hill, we made a groove in the snow to deliver the board to the bush. You'd dart down the slope, drop into the rut. When the board hit the trunk, you'd go flying, head over heels, over the bushes. You'd fold into a somersault, land on your rump. That was the best.

Before long, we were hot-dogging it, copping a christie into the rut, adding a twist, double flips, the whole nine yards. It was all about style and distance. The faster you were flying when you drilled the trunk, the farther you'd fly over the bush. It was beyond fun, pure wintertime ecstasy. You'd pray for snow, listen to the school cancellations, wax the board and head for the hills.

The snow fell deep back then, covered the bleachers at Angel Field. We'd fly right over the seats, launch off the wall, wipe out on the track that circled the football field, get up and do it again, get up the courage and go for distance, mark the landings with lines in the snow.

Without bindings, you'd wipe out on jumps so my brother Dougie mick-rigged bungee cords to hold your boots, pretty much invented the snowboard right then and there. With your feet attached, you could land without wiping. We built jumps on the hills, had all kinds of newfangled fun.

Years later, they started the Snurfer Nationals, something like that, up at a little ski area just north of Kalamazoo, Pando up by Grand Rapids. The competition wasn't much, the Nationals tag just a joke, just a few fools showed up, but it was the only time you could take a Snurfer on a ski area, ride up the rope-tow and race down the hill. It was like skateboard-riding at the parking ramp, taking the elevator to save up your energy. If you have the technology, you take advantage of it.

Snurfers went fast, would have left snowboards in the dust if you didn't wipe out. You could slalom a bit, but mostly it was a dive-bomb down the hill, schussing to the finish line. Snurfers weren't really made for the ski slopes. Like running a marathon, making it to the end was an accomplishment on its own. If you could do that, you were a winner in my book.

My older brother Mike had learned his lesson from a dirt-bike accident, decided to wear his ice-hockey helmet, was the only one that did, started a tradition that probably saved the skulls of countless snowboarders in the decades that followed. Jake Burton knew what he was doing, showed up one year with a new design, a team of riders, the snowboard had arrived.

Over time, the course changed and riding Snurfers became outdated, was like trying to drive rail-dragsters on a figure-eight track. They went good in the straight-aways but were bound to roll in the curves. I never thought that one day they'd let boards on the lifts every day of the week.

Anyway, that's history and I was there at the beginning. If it sounds like I'm bragging, it's because that's what I'm doing. I'm a Michigander, that's what we do. We bled the blood, broke the bones, earned our bragging rights.

Bob Winch
(K. College)

Winch Industries

Hot Wheels Winternationals
(Bob Winch & Andrew Smith)

STOMPING GROUND

I was conceived in Cleveland, born in New York, moved to Michigan before kindergarten, in the late Sixties when all that junk was going on, the riots over in Detroit, that war in Vietnam, Woodstock and Kennedy and all that, but I didn't give a rat's ass. We had our own riots, on the North Side and down at Old Central, and I thought that sounded pretty kick, but I didn't go there, was just a little kid, mostly just thought about Evel Knievel, what he was doing, what he'd do if he were me.

At first, we lived in this run-down house on the Northeast Side of Kalamazoo, until my dad got a kick deal on a rental and moved us to the other side of downtown. That's where I spent most of my life, right where I belonged, on the West Side of the city. That side was the best side around, stretched out for miles and miles, but our house was close to the center of town. West Main Elementary was about a mile away in the other direction.

Those blocks around my school and my house were my stomping ground, had everybody and everything that mattered, the sinkhole grove behind our house neck-high with leaves in the fall, vines to swing on all year, the high dive at the swimming pool, the student ghetto crawling with all kinds of miniskirts and pretty girls, the graveyard full of ghosts and tombstones, Henderson Park and Angel Field, chocolate-covered ants at Tiffany's Party Store, fifteen-cent cherry Cokes at Carousel Ice Cream, indoor miniature golf at Duffy's, pinball arcade under the colored lights at Tony's Pizza.

Maybe it's just the Catholic in me, don't wish for what you don't have and all that, but if I could have grown up any place at any time, I wouldn't change a thing. I was the middle kid, like most kids back then, didn't have to tell anybody where I was going, just jumped on my Stingray and went. I pedaled or hoofed to school, back home every afternoon, cut through Lewis's every time.

In the summer, they had the program in the school yard. You didn't have to sign up, just went when you wanted, left when you felt like it, played tetherball and tabletop hockey, board games and Ping Pong, swinging on the swing-set, scaling the monkey-bars.

Sometimes kids that I didn't know would show up, visiting for the summer, this tomboy named Cricket who smoked Kool cigarettes and could cream everybody at tetherball. She meant business, had a mean arm on her, could wrap the swing around the pole without even trying, had been in juvie, was a lot older than me, almost grown up, twelve or thirteen, and there was this girl Sheila from a divorced family. She came to Kalamazoo in the summer, lived in California the rest of the time.

Back then, parents didn't split up much, not in Michigan, so I was interested in that Sheila girl, and I couldn't believe there was a place that didn't even have winter in the wintertime, where all the girls probably looked a lot like Sheila. She was a stone-cold fox, the definition of sex appeal. If they have that word in the dictionary, they have to put a picture of Sheila in there, her and her tanned skin and sparkling blue eyes, her blonde hair parted in the middle, straight down her back, her yellow tank top and matching miniskirt, her California underwear in clear view when she'd twirl on the monkey-bars. I never said a word to her but I loved her a lot. She gave me my first boner.

Actually, Sheila wasn't my first. My first one came from a college girl, this one on my *Detroit Free Press* paper route. I had to deliver those papers before the sun came up, was always freezing my balls off, had that strap digging in my shoulder, especially with the inserts on Sunday morning. But I made money and I had the college on my route, and that made it worth it. I'd rogue Milk Shake candy bars from the vending machine, reach my scrawny arm up the chute, finger loose the chocolate and nougat. And I got to go in the girls' dorm. Boys weren't allowed there, but I was just a little kid so they said it was okay. I could just leave the bundle in the TV room, but I liked roaming around, watching all the ladies in their pj's, some of them wearing almost nothing.

"SALLY. PUT ON A TOP."

"How come?"

"You're gettin' that little boy all excited."

"Oh." She put her arms over her boobs. "I thought that was a girl. Our little paper girl."

"Not even." Usually that made me mad, but that time I didn't mind it. I was like a spy in the dorm of dames. I'd pocket my mittens and yank off my hat, wave hello to all of them. They all seemed to like me, but they had to face facts. My heart belonged to the girl at the end of the hall.

I'd stop by the bathroom, look in the mirror and try to look my best, hold my hat in my lap, go down and knock on the doorway to my true love, hand-deliver the paper to her bedroom. She was like a girl-next-door version of Raquel Welch, with long flowing hair the color of caramel, skin soft as marshmallows and a perfect potbelly. She always hugged me the second she saw me, thought I was the cutest boy she'd ever seen. She told me that and I believed it, had no reason to doubt her. She was almost naked almost every time, her nightshirt hanging off her boobs, her deep bellybutton always showing. Down below that, she had her see-through underpants, a big furry critter packed in there. It was so close, I could have reached out and petted it.

"Hey you." She'd lift my chin with her finger. "Whaddya doin'?"

"I dunno." Just looking.

"Uh-huh." Sometimes she'd whittle her finger, shame-shame me, maybe knowing what I was thinking. She'd say to wait while she got decent.

"Okay." I always wanted to tell her that she always looked more than decent to me. But I'd just wait in the hall and rub the ball on my hat.

She'd come back in a bathrobe, take my hand and bring me into her bedroom, unbutton my coat and rub my sore shoulders, make me roll up my sleeves and show her my muscles.

"You've got a lot of scars."

"I got this one right out there."

"Oh." She looked out the window. "On the wall?"

"Yep. I got it just last summer."

"I knew you then."

"I know." That's one reason I did it. "I flew right past your bedroom."

"You fell off the wall?"

"Nope." It was only high as the high-dive at the pool. "I jumped off it."

"How come?"

"I got dared." I'm a daredevil so I did it. "It's like skydivin'."

"But you got hurt."

"I feel good now."

"You have to be more careful."

"It was a cinch."

"Oh my gosh." She rubbed her finger over the scar. "At least you didn't break any bones."

"Just my toe."

"You broke your toe?"

"Don't tell nobody."

"You never told anybody?"

"I didn't even cry."

"That's so sad." That's what she told me. She thought it was a big deal that boys weren't allowed to cry when they'd get hurt. She thought that was a problem, that society had problems like that. She knew a lot about society. She was from some other place far away, maybe Minnesota or Arizona, and she believed that boys have feelings and should feel free to cry, free to be you and me and all that. That didn't make sense to me, but I didn't mind taking off my shoes and socks and showing her my bent toe. I would have showed her everything if she wanted to see that.

"I'd have to pull down my pants to show you that one."

"You better not do that."

"I don't mind."

"People might get ideas."

"Okay." I had tons of ideas too. She told me that I was pretty tough, and more importantly, I was a good listener. She said a man like that is hard to find, and I believed every word she said. I would have sat on her love seat all day if she wanted that, listening to her tell me about all her hassles, and society's hang-ups, nodding my chin and thinking about the future. I knew she had a head start, but I'd done the mathematics, that wouldn't matter when we got older. When I was sixteen, she'd still be in her twenties, both of us old enough to get married. If she didn't want to do that, we could always shack up. I'd seen it on *Love, American Style*, knew it could happen to me.

When I asked my cootie-catcher about our future, it opened up to good news, had me looking up. I couldn't wait to get older, enjoyed being little in the meantime. When she'd hug me, I'd reach right around her big hips and touch her butt. It was right there, what could I do.

For Christmas, she came to the door in her holiday outfit, a dinky top that barely covered her up, matching underpants and fuzzy slippers. When she gave me a hug, her belly was warm like fresh bread from a potbelly stove, smelling like something good, like spiced cider cooking on that stove. She invited me in before she even got decent, sat me down on her love seat and gave me my present.

"Close your eyes."

"Okay." Of course, I was peeking. "I'm ready for it."

"It's nothing big."

"That's okay." Like they say, it ain't the size of the box, it's what's in it. It's what you get that counts. And that was the best present of my whole life, maybe even better than Rock 'Em Sock 'Em Robots. It was a sampler box of Fanny Farmer chocolates.

"You like it?"

"I love it." And it wasn't just because I loved candy. I loved her too, and I knew where our relationship was headed. If I were just a little kid to her, she would have gotten me a chocolate Santa Claus, a candy cane or something like that, but she didn't. She got me grown-up candy, and then I knew what was going to happen. Someday, we might get married. I could hardly wait.

"I'll be tossin' the tassel after next semester."

"Oh." I'd like to see that.

"You know what I mean?"

"Nope." I had no idea.

"I'm graduating in the spring."

"Okay." I wasn't sure what that meant, but it sounded good. "Good for you."

"That means I'll be leaving."

"Oh." That didn't sound so good. But that spring, she tossed that tassel, left me there with nothing but my memories. I had a pain in my heart. And something else growing in my cut-offs.

GOING BLIND

I had a big boner problem that summer. It was hard to ignore, almost like a stray dog. Once you pet it, it'll keep coming back. It really wants you to do that. That's the way it seemed to me.

When I first started rubbing it, I'd just get that good-good feeling, but one night some stuff squirted right out of it. That scared the heck out of me. I thought it was pus or something, thought I'd done something wrong, thought I'd gotten an infection from touching myself too much. I knew I'd gotten that wart on my hand from doing that, but this was even worse.

When I went to get that wart electrocuted from my palm, the doctor asked me if I'd been playing with toads, but I knew he was just kidding around. I knew what he meant. He knew what I was doing. Since he didn't call the fuzz on me, I thought about telling him about the infection in my thing, but the nurse was in the room. I figured maybe if I stopped, the infection would clear up.

But it wasn't easy to quit doing that. That made my balls hurt, and the pus looked worse when I'd wait, so I decided doing it a lot might be the best way to clear up the problem. The infection must have spread to my balls, and I had to get rid of it one way or another. If you've got a big pimple, you pop it. If another one pops up, you get that one too. It was at least worth a try. I'd get out my magazines and hump my pillow all the time, get that feeling and want to feel that again.

When the infection wouldn't go away, I finally decided that stuff must be the junk that makes girls get pregnant. That didn't make me feel that much better because I was still doing something wrong. It was supposed to go in a girl's thing or something, and I was squirting it on my pillow. So I made some rules about doing it, would never daydream about real-live girls that I loved because that didn't seem right. Usually, I'd think about this foxy lady in my skiing magazine.

That chick was something else, helped me make love out of almost nothing. She didn't have to do much. She was drinking tequila and her blouse was unbuttoned. Pretty soon, my pillow looked a lot like her. I'd slide my hand up her miniskirt and you can imagine the rest. You just need a good imagination. Mine was running away with me, taking me to places I'd never been to before.

I also used Barbie dolls. But they weren't objects like you might think. I was making love to their minds, not just their boobs and stuff. I'd have long and important conversations with them before anything happened, hold them out and squint to make them look fuzzy, to make them look more real, like girls at night. I'd pretend they were walking down the street, coming at me.

"Hello," I'd say to black-power Barbie. "What's hap'nin?"

"What it is."

"I'm tellin' you."

"You know what I'm sayin'?"

"I do know that."

"That's a fact."

"Fact of the matter. What about that?"

"That's all I'm sayin'."

"I heard that." We had an understanding. "So how you doin'?"

"I'm fine," she'd say.

"I know. You'd have to be blind in your eyes to not see that." She'd smile at me and after we rapped for a while, the yellow spaghetti straps of her sun dress would fall off her brown shoulders.

"You fuh'na go blind you keep doin' that."

"I know." But it's worth it. "I can't help myself."

"You need some help with that?"

"I could use a hand." You can guess the rest. It's too embarrassing to tell the details.

HOT PANTS & HALTER-TOPS

Once a few years later, I thought I was going to finally get some, some of whatever girls had. I was going to get it if I could, from a girl named Julie M. I knew she had to have it. She had panty lines in her hot pants, spaghetti-strap tan lines over her bare shoulders, brown hair the color of hot fudge, always wore teensy-weensy white outfits to show off her suntan and everything she had. She smelled like vanilla ice cream and looked like a million bucks, had a cute face and real boobs, two big scoops of French vanilla bouncing under her terry-cloth tube-top. And she'd let older boys put their hands in there. And other places too. That's what I'd heard. I took their words for it, didn't want to smell their fingers. They might have been fibbing, but I had to find out.

I spent a lot of time that summer looking at her school picture, reading the cursive writing on the back, *I hope we get to know each other better since we live so close, don't be so quiet, stay sweet and gain weight, Julie M.* After she wrote that, I spent my earnings on nothing but sweets and candy, banana splits and cherry Cokes, anything high in calories, stole all the Crunch Berries and hit the supper table early, daydreamed about Julie all the time, rescuing her from all kinds of emergencies, from forest fires and atomic wars, laser beams and aliens from outer space, tornados and car accidents too. Maybe one day, she'd be playing hopscotch in her hot pants and halter-top, wouldn't notice that mushroom cloud rising on the horizon, or maybe a Mack truck was coming right at her. The driver was super fat and had a Big Mac attack, or maybe a heart attack, couldn't hit the brakes. The truck was out of control, about to hit her, so I'd grab her just in time, tackle her to the side of the road. Then I'd be her hero and she'd give me a wet kiss and everything.

I'd also wait by her house, hide by the corner and start walking down the sidewalk if she came out, just pretend it was by accident that we ran into each other.

One day, I invited her over and she came. When we were hoofing to my house, I asked her if she wanted to go to the fair that night and she said she did. It was like my daydream had come true, walking down the sidewalk for the whole wide world to see, stepping on cracks like we didn't have a worry in the world, like we had nothing to hide, me in my tank top and cord cut-offs, her sporting her white hot pants and a white-denim vest with buttons in the front and her bellybutton showing.

And when she got to my bedroom, she seemed to like it, checked out all my drawings of skulls, my black-light posters and my little stack of eight-tracks. "You like the Alice Cooper Group?"

"Yeah." Of course.

"You know how to play guitar?"

"Yeah." A little bit.

"Cool." She handed it to me. "Play me a song."

"Okay." I sat on my beanbag, took a deep breath, played the only tune I knew.

"That's 'Smoke on the Water.'"

"Yeah." I felt good that she recognized it, that she knew that song and that I'd played it good enough for her to know what I was playing.

"Everybody knows that one."

"Oh." Bummer.

"You know any others?"

"I'm workin' on some." Or I figured I'd start. "I'll play 'em for you. If you want. Later. When I get better."

"Okay." She waited in my room when I had to wash the dishes.

I telephoned Harley to tell him the news, did my chores as fast as I could, but when I came back, Julie had already looked through my stash of *Oui* and *Penthouse* that I'd found on the Boy Scout paper drive. She must have looked under my mattress, was on my bed, resting on her belly and looking at those magazines. I was hoping she hadn't looked at that one. But she had.

"How come you pasted my school picture on this page? Over this naked girl's face? Huh?"

"What?" Oh no. "I didn't do that."

"Yeah right." I thought she'd be ticked off, but she wasn't. She thought it was funny, hopefully didn't know why I'd done that. We went to the fair.

It all seemed to go good. I didn't try to do anything, but I planned to, to do something. I just wasn't sure what. We rode some rides and sat on the ground to make the world stop spinning and when we got up, I tried to slap the grass stains from her hot pants and that made her giggle and laugh, made me feel good because I'd touched her butt and she didn't seem to mind that.

After that I played this game, chucked the darts at the balloons until I won the giant teddy bear. I gave it to her, figured I was doing pretty good. She seemed happy as can be, hugged the stuffed animal, twirled around with the arms of the bear dangling over her shoulders, her outfit shining in the midway lights, and I felt like it couldn't be going better. But then she met this older guy.

She told me to hold the bear while she went somewhere with him, said she'd be back in a minute, but she was lying. I waited a long time before I realized that.

I ended up hoofing home alone, just me and the bear. I brought it to bed, closed my eyes, pretended it was Julie, fell asleep with the bear in my arms, woke up to Harley yelling at me.

"HEY WINCH. You awake?"

"Yeah." I am now. "Whaddya want?"

"What happened? You get anywhere last night? Make it to second base?"

"Maybe." I never understood which base meant what anyway. "Maybe it ain't none of your business."

"Struck out, eh?"

"Maybe. Maybe it's none of your business. I told you."

"You sleepin' with a teddy bear?"

"Not even. I won it for her. She forgot to take it home."

"How come there's a hole in the crotch?"

"Who knows." I wouldn't put your finger in there. "Put it down."

"You were humpin' this teddy bear, weren't you?"

"Yeah right."

PART TWO:
CHICKS & TRIPS

HEATWAVE

That summer it was hot as the temperature under your tongue when you're sick, or even when you ain't sick, it's still hot inside you. Your guts are pretty hot if you think about it and under the blankets it gets sticky and it's no good trying to sleep in even though there's no school for months so you kneel on your bed and look out the window, and every Tuesday morning at about 10:52 AM the bookmobile stopped across from my house. I had never been there but I watched Valerie Pratt barefoot down her front yard in her brown corduroy cut-offs. She tied her chocolate-milk hair into a braid as she went along, like she had just gotten out of bed and was walking to the bathroom.

I'd seen her all year standing at the bus stop and smacking the tetherball in the playground but I'd never seen her with her hair down. I didn't really care about most girls my own age and that stuff too much because I was just in the sixth grade, actually seventh because sixth was over, but you don't really feel like a seventh-grader until junior high starts and I had a long time before it started.

Valerie always stayed awhile in the truck and there were no windows to see what she was doing in there, but finally the door opened and she jumped off and waved goodbye to the driver. It was too hot to even camp on the floor looking at Wacky Pack stickers, so after Valerie walked home, I put on some cut-offs, booked downstairs for a giant bowl of King Vitamin. I emptied the box but my brother had already got the prize so I stood at the kitchen window crunching on the cereal and drooling milk and wondering what Valerie did all day. She probably stayed in bed, on her belly with her bare feet in the air and reading her bundle of books. She probably had air-conditioning.

I figured what the heck and wiped the milk from my mouth, went outside and across the street, ran over to the shade of the bookmobile because the pavement was burning on my feet. The shadow hadn't really cooled the ground yet so I figured that I might as well go in.

It was weird stepping into that bus without any shoes because on a school bus they don't let you do that, but Valerie hadn't been wearing shoes and I didn't see any signs about no shoes. I hate those signs when you're walking around and want an ice-cream drumstick from Harding's Friendly Market but you can't get one because all you got on is cut-offs, but the driver lady smiled at me and said "Come on in, young man," so I figured it was okay. She was a pretty lady with a blonde ponytail, not at all how I had pictured her even though I hadn't really pictured her.

I had always wondered what it was like in that bookmobile and let me tell you, it's nothing like a school bus. It's got air-conditioning and it's like a big camper full of books, kind of like a library but smaller and cleaner. I was pretty cold without even a shirt on.

The driver lady not only drove the truck but she was a librarian lady too, and she showed me around because it was just me and her in there and I think she was happy to have the company instead of being alone with the Dewey Decimal System and books and junk. Her name was Beth and she told me her name like I was almost a grownup too. She was one of those older people who actually listen to you talk and sometimes I'll just keep on talking if someone will listen.

Finally I shut up and when she started talking, I wasn't really listening to her, I was more thinking about how I could probably marry her if I was older. If she had a car wreck with the bookmobile, I could save her just in time before it blew up to smithereens and then we'd maybe get married when I got older.

I think maybe she knew what I was thinking because she smiled and it was a little weird and I started scratching my palm because she had all her clothes on and I was in that little library with her and feeling almost naked. But she was pretty nice for a librarian, not too old like most librarians and she seemed interested in me and especially the books. She was one of those ladies that loved books. I almost forgot it was the inside of a truck.

Then all of a sudden the door opened and I was thinking who the heck is this, probably Harley or something and he's going to tease me about going to the bookmobile, but he can't say nothing because he's here too. But no, it was Valerie, Valerie Pratt. What the heck did she come back for?

There was no back door except that one that said Emergency Only, and I didn't think the librarian lady would think my itchy palm was an emergency. Valerie was wearing those brown cut-offs as usual and a yellow shirt unbuttoned all the way and underneath a tank-top underwear shirt, and I was wearing nothing but my cut-offs like I already told you.

"Hey, Beth."

"Hey, Val. Long time, no see."

"Yeah." They were kidding around because Valerie was just there. They didn't know I knew that, but it seemed like they knew something that I didn't. "Hey you."

"What?" I wondered what she wanted.

"I didn't know you went to the bookmobile."

"Yeah," I said, or something stupid like that. I wanted to tell her not to tell anybody, but I didn't say anything and she started coming at me and the librarian lady went back to the front compartment like she wanted to leave us alone. I knew Valerie was going to get really near to me like she always does and I didn't want her to get too close because I didn't brush my teeth, I never brush my teeth in the summer, but I'd just got done with that mixing bowl of King Vitamin and one time last year I got on the school bus and Pudley said, *Hey, your breath stinks like Frosted Flakes*, and Valerie was right there that day and heard him say that and I felt like dying or something, like beating the crap out of Pudley. He was always getting on my nerves.

Anyway Valerie came right up to me and trapped me against the books. I couldn't go anywhere without pushing her so I licked the King Vitamin from my teeth and just stood there. She was so close I could smell the Honeycombs on her mouth.

"Wow, your freckles really come out in the summer."

"Yeah." Big deal.

"Look at mine." She turned and let her shirt fall off her shoulder and lifted her braid. "See?"

"Yeah." Freckles were everywhere.

When we stepped outside, the heat of the day was thick as Campbell's Alphabet Soup and I wanted to climb back into that truck, take Valerie with me and we could spend the whole day with her showing me books, and me behind her pretending not to look at her bra strap and maybe counting all the freckles on her back.

"You been workin' on your summer packet?"

"Yeah right." That'll be the day.

"I'll catch you later."

"Okay." Later.

"That's a good book. I bet you'll like it."

"Yeah. Okay." But I wasn't planning on reading it. It was summer, there were tons of other junk to do. "The pool's comin' tonight."

"Oh yeah?"

"Yeah. Every Tuesday night. You never been?" I knew she hadn't because I'd go every week and never saw her there.

"Never."

"It's tons of fun. And free. Y'oughta go."

"Maybe." That's exactly what she said, maybe. Girls say stuff like that.

*

So that night just after supper, the traveling swimming pool parked across the street, almost the same spot as the bookmobile. It had to go tons of places, and it came to our neighborhood the last and it's just a big tank on the back of a truck, but it's still a swimming pool. I'd been waiting since dessert so as soon as I saw it coming, I took off, dumped the green beans from my pocket and splashed right in. Even though it'd been to lots of places before us, I still liked being first.

I stood in the water with my snorkeling mask on top of my head, pretending to watch the water drip on the sidewalk, but I was mostly watching Valerie's house. I didn't know if she'd show up or not, didn't know if she even liked swimming in a pool that had been to tons of other places, maybe even down to those big buildings by Meijer's Thrifty Acres where tons of black kids and white kids that talk like black kids live. I don't care about that, even if a kid without ears or something had been swimming in it, but some people do and she could have been one of them.

But she did finally come out of her house wearing nothing but her brown cut-offs and a yellow towel over her shoulders so you couldn't see her bikini top and I thought for a second she wasn't wearing one. Some of the little kids go without tops, but she wasn't a little kid. I hate to tell you, but she had boobs already. It made me scratch my palm just thinking about her coming to the pool bare-chested. I don't know what I would have done if that had happened.

Her feet smacked the sidewalk when she got near, and then I could see that she was wearing a top. It was orange as an orange, or more like two oranges, and I pretended not to watch when she dropped her cut-offs to her feet and kicked them against a tree. She turned around with her arms crossed over her chest and I slipped the mask over my face.

I hid on the bottom of the pool, just sitting there watching her naked legs step down the ladder. I scuba-dived over and bit her foot just to give her a good scare, and it worked because she kicked me in the teeth. I pretended it didn't hurt and she pretended that she

55

didn't think I was weird for biting her foot. I don't know why I do stuff like that, but she didn't seem to mind.

"The water's warm, ain't it?"

"Of course." I knew that a long time ago. "What took you so long?"

"My mom made me wait. She's afraid I'll get a cramp and drown."

"It's not even deep enough to drown."

"You'd save me anyway. Right?"

"I doubt it," I said and I dunked her.

We played freeze tag and took turns closing our eyes and playing Marco Polo, and she sat on my shoulders when we played chicken war with Mark and Lisa. I had to hold Valerie's legs so she wouldn't fall off and the bottom of her bikini was on the back of my neck. I was glad I was in water for a reason I can't talk about, and she stood on my shoulders as I bent down into the water and sprung up and flung her into the air until the lady said *None of that*, and the Ramquist twins teased us about sitting in a tree, *K-I-S-S-I-N-G*, but who cares about that. We weren't going to get married, weren't doing anything, just swam and stuff, stayed in the water until our fingers were white as newborn babies and wrinkled as an old person. Until the lady blew her whistle.

Valerie put on her shorts right in front of me, and it almost seemed like she was wearing an orange bra and right next to me getting dressed, which must have made me stare at her.

"What?"

"Nothin'." I tried not to look but she had cut the cut-offs pretty short with the pockets sticking out the bottom. And that's all she was wearing, that and the top part of her bikini.

"Whaddya lookin' at?"

"I said nothin'." That's what I said, but I was wondering what she'd look like if she untied her braid, with that and without a shirt, but I looked away and all of us stood in our towels and watched the lady cover the pool and listened to it slosh away as she drove off leaving just puddles and nothing else except the wet footprints on the sidewalk when we ran to Henderson Park.

We played ditch 'em and Valerie hadn't played with us before so I showed her some good hiding spots and we played until dark when all the little kids had to go to bed, and before Valerie had to go in, I sat with her on the tree trunk by the seesaw.

"What's this?" She touched my cheek and looked at her finger. "You got hurt?"

"No. I smeared fireflies on me."

"How come?"

"It makes your face glow in the dark."

"Uh-huh."

"Are they still glowin'?"

"No." She wiped off her finger. "It's just bug guts."

"Oh." I wiped them off and we tried to count the rings in the tree and she brushed off the wood with the tip of her braid and showed me how you could tell by the rings when it was winter and summer and even if it was a good year. "How come you always wear that braid?"

"You don't like it?"

"Beats me."

"You've never seen me with my hair down, have you?"

"No," I said, but that was a lie. I didn't want her to know that I spied on her.

"Wanna see?"

"I don't care." That was another lie. She took the marbles from her hair and untied the braid and when she shook her head, the hair fell like a bucket of chocolate milk over her shoulders.

"Whaddya think?"

"I dunno." But I did know. She looked like a fox, with her hair like that and I wanted to tell her that, but instead I pulled a strand out of her head.

"Ouch." She said that but she smiled. "You wanna hear a story?"

"I guess."

"Okay." She pulled the paperback from her back pocket and sat so close to me that our butts were touching and I could smell the chlorine and strawberry shampoo in her hair. She put the book on her lap and read about something but I wasn't really listening. I just looked down at the book and noticed that the wet of her bikini bottom showed through the corduroy of her shorts.

*

Now it's almost the beginning of junior high and when I went away to sport camp, a lot of stuff happened when I was gone, and none of it was good. First, they decided to not bring the pool around anymore, for some dumbbell reason. And Valerie started going with Donnie McCray. He's got a brand-new mini-bike that he didn't even make himself. He just bought it at a store, and he's tons older than her, going in eighth grade, so it doesn't seem right. I feel like socking him in the face because he's probably not as tough as he thinks he is. I didn't even know that she liked him, or that he liked her. I don't think he even likes books. I feel like telling her that.

I wish I hadn't gone to sport camp and had so much fun because if I'd stayed here, Valerie's house might have caught on fire and I could have crawled in her window and rescued her and then went back and saved her goldfish before they got boiled and maybe even saved her mom and dad from burning up, and then I'd go back to Valerie and lift her off the grass with her maybe in a white nightgown and slippers so they could take our picture for the newspaper, and then I'd be her hero and she'd wet-kiss me and we'd probably be going together right now. Maybe we'd be sitting on this curb instead of how it really is, with me sitting here alone, waiting for that dumb bookmobile.

NORTHGLADE

I went to West Main Elementary for five years, all but third and fifth grade, but I don't really remember much, just looking out the second-story window, watching all the grownups and dropouts across the four-lane, half-day kindergarten kids getting cherry Cokes and banana splits at Carousel Ice Cream, housewives grocery shopping at Harding's Friendly Market, picking up pork chops at Main Street Butcher Shop, me stuck in school, waiting for recess, wiping the hay fever from my nose, smearing snot across my sleeve, hoping nobody noticed.

In third grade, I got bussed down to the North Side. That was in the 1970s and it must have been the first year of bussing in Michigan, but I didn't know about that, just walked down to the corner and got on the yellow bus. They dropped me off at Northglade Elementary.

For most white kids, it was probably the first time they'd set foot on the North Side, but it wasn't for me. When I was four years old, I'd gotten lost on the way home from the Art Center. I'd gone there in the morning, got dropped off in the Winch Wagon, made some snakes out of clay, was supposed to walk home, use the map my mom made me to get there. But I was only a preschooler, got the drawing all wrong, was supposed to make a left at the first corner, but on the map it looked like the last street. That's what I thought. I walked all morning, waiting to find that T in the road.

By the afternoon, I'd hoofed for hours and miles, all through downtown, made it to the North Side. It was flipped out, all the people had turned to chocolate. But I kept on walking. I tried turning left on some streets but they didn't bring me to any place I knew, so I'd go back to the street on my map, hoping pretty soon I'd run into that T.

I knew what it would look like because we lived at the top of a T in the road. People would miss the turn and drive right into our house, wake you up and make you think it was the night before doomsday or something like that. You'd go downstairs to see the blood and guts. So I knew you couldn't miss a T in the road without running into a house. But the road just kept going.

When the chocolate kids went in for supper, I got hungry in my belly. I felt like bawling but I held it in, just like I was holding that big poop that was poking out of my butt. I tried to keep it in, but I farted a big one and the big turd slipped out. I went in the bushes and scooped it out. I had BM on my hands but I kept walking down the sidewalk, still waiting for that T in the road.

I'd been walking down Westnedge, the business loop of Highway 131, but I didn't know that then, just knew something wasn't right when I reached the end of the sidewalk. By that time, it was almost nighttime and I'd been walking all day, and the houses were gone, the highway stretching out in front of me. I stood there awhile, wondering what to do.

But I was a smart little stinker, took a U-turn and followed the same route, the same road but going the other way, walked through downtown and pretended not to hear people when they talked to me because it was dark and I didn't feel like getting kidnapped. I didn't even care about not stepping on the cracks anymore, and finally I made it to the Art Center and decided to start over.

This time I looked at the street signs, didn't know how to read yet but I recognized that first one from somewhere. It was the one on the map. I took a left on that and after a while, I realized the mistake I'd made. And actually, it was really my mom's fault because she hadn't learned how to draw right, but I started recognizing some of the buildings, Dairy Queen and other stuff, the sewer creek and the railroad tracks. After a while, I was walking up to my house.

I'd been missing since the morning, and Mom and Dad were a bit worried, had called the cops. The policemen were waiting in my yard, pistols hanging from their belts, weird looks on their faces. I wanted to run to my mom but they wouldn't let me, had to talk to me about something. I was thinking, couldn't this wait until later, maybe tomorrow or next week or something, but they had to talk to me right then. I didn't understand it at all. I was really mad at them. "Whaddya want?"

"Were you scared?"

"Whaddya think?" I pooped my pants, didn't I? "I fell in dog poop."

"You were running away?"

"I GOT LOST." I wasn't even in kindergarten yet, why would I run away? For what reason would I do that? That didn't make sense to me. My mom and dad were standing right there in front of the house, but the police wouldn't let me go. I couldn't hold it in no more, started bawling.

They finally got done writing in their pads, let me go to my house. We weren't a hugging family, but my mom saved me a plate from dinner and made me a bath and even my brothers were nice to me, didn't even tease me about reeking like BM. After I stashed my underwear and took a bath, I ate that meat-loaf supper like it was going out of style. I gobbled up my food, didn't even pocket the green beans. It was a good adventure I had that day, but I was glad to be home.

Anyway, so I'd been to the North Side before they started bussing, that's what I started to tell you before I remembered about getting lost, figured I had to tell you about that. And actually I'd been to the North Side tons of times, used to hoof down to Meijer's Thrifty Acres to get battleship models and junk, got along fine when they sent me to Northglade Elementary.

Of course, sometimes Candy Brown would chase me around and pin me on the ground and pull my hair and kiss me on the mouth, but she'd give me back my milk money if I promised not to tell and for the most part, I liked it there, they had a petting zoo in the playground, real farm animals, goats or something. And we had special classes.

I took French with this foxy college lady, got to leave class, learned how to count to a hundred and say hello to men and ladies, how you doing, and all that. And I got along with the black kids, for the most part. But some of them would sock me in the face for no reason.

Maybe it was because I was white, and because I was playing with black kids, but I didn't even think of that until years later. Back then, I didn't think like that. They were prejudiced, but I didn't care about that. I was just a kid. Kids are people too, but I guess they didn't know that. But that was just a few of them. I knew that. And most of the kids were cool, spitting goobers and cussing insults, rowdy and loudmouthed. They were like me, but with chocolate skin.

At lunch recess, we'd have wrestling matches, class against class, just the jungle-bunny boys and big-boned Candy Brown and me and my friend Karl Fugate, this kraut-American kid from my neighborhood. At my old school, they wouldn't let us wrestle, so it was a blast, sort of like a free-for-all but it had rules too. If you got chucked to the ground, you were considered dead and had to wait until the battle was over, until everybody from one class was out. It went good until one day this kid from my class, Odell Snell was his name and he joined the other team. That didn't seem right to me because it was supposed to be class against class so it ticked me off when he did that.

When the game started, I made a b-line to him and chucked him on the ground. That's part of the game, but I think he knew I wasn't just playing around. I was really mad at him.

Anyway, Odell Snell didn't even pretend he was dead after I threw him down, and the day after that happened, he got some of his buddies to jump me. They all pinned me down, had it all planned, got me where the teachers couldn't see us.

Then this kid stepped out of the bushes, this boy that didn't go to school much, just showed up at recess sometimes. He had something wrong with his head, had been in a car wreck, or was just born with a deformed face. You didn't even like looking at him.

Anyway, Odell and them were holding me down, waiting for that deformed kid to show up. And when he came out of the bushes, he had something in his hand, part of an old bike, that bar that crushes your nuts when you wipe out. It was from an old Schwinn, shaped like a caveman's club. I tried to get loose, but them kids were holding me down and that deformed one just stood above me, thumping that bar into his palm. He didn't hit me with it, was probably just trying to scare me. But he did stomp my head, lifted his old Buster Brown and bashed in my face pretty good.

The next thing I remember was lying there by myself, half knocked out. I'd been socked plenty before that, wiped out tons of times, but I'd never gotten knocked out. It ain't like fights on TV, it takes a lot of stomping to do that. When I came to my senses, I got up and headed toward class.

Pretty soon, everyone was running up to me, asking what happened. I was trying my best to not start crying. I wasn't a crybaby, but I was just in third grade and I was hurt pretty bad. Some teacher brought me to the office and after the door shut, I started bawling. I admit that.

The nurse splashed that smelly Merthiolate junk on my wounds and wrapped gauze around my head. Then I was supposed to go around the school and tattle on everybody involved. That red mercury junk was still burning my skin and my face was bleeding, I was a mess, just wanted to go home, but they wouldn't let me. That made me really mad that they did that. I felt like those grownups didn't know anything about how a kid feels when something like that happens.

To make it even worse, Lisa Wilbur was in one of the rooms where they brought me. I knew she was in there, and she just happened to be the cutest girl in the whole wide world, in the whole universe probably. I had been in love with her for about a million years, at least since the beginning of third grade. I had never loved a girl the way I loved her and I had to stand in the doorway while she sat at her desk staring right at me. My face was wrapped up in gauze and dripping red with Merthiolate, blood and embarrassment, and my belly was in a knot. I was so mad, more at the grownups than at those kids who'd beat me up. I never tattled on any of them.

Finally they gave up trying to get me to do that, and the next day I was bandaged up with fresh wrappings, looking like I had a mummy face but back to the wrestling game.

And Odell Snell never again went to play with the other team. That was wrong, we all knew that. Just because your name is Odell Snell, that don't mean you can do that. That ain't right. If Odell Snell had gone to the other team again, I would have probably chucked him down just like before. Even in a free-for-all, there are rules. Everybody should follow them.

FOURTH GRADE

The next year they sent me back to West Main Elementary, for fourth grade, and I remember we had a student teacher that had pixie hair parted on the side and pinned back with butterfly barrettes. She smelled like Jolly Ranchers, looked like a blonde version of Karen Valentine from *Love, American Style*, and that spin-off show *Room 222*. She'd rescue me from Candy Brown and kneel by my desk and put her arm around my shoulder, put smiley faces on my book reports. When we got our class picture, I wrote *MY WIFE* on the back behind her portrait. I loved her to death, even admitted it to my best friend Ricky Poling, told him I was going to marry her.

"You wish."

"Yep." I did. When she went back to college, she took my heart with her, slipped it in a manila folder and left with it. I kissed her picture and pinned it to the paneling above my bed.

Of course, after a while I realized that Debby Donalds was the one I really loved. She was really pretty, that's what she was, pretty with a capital P. One time, she came to school in a see-through miniskirt and they made her go home and change. Her dad raced cars and had to come get her. She didn't come back until the next day and I wondered what had happened, figured she must have been embarrassed. That's all I remember about fourth grade. It's something I'll never forget.

THE BIGGEST LITTLE CITY IN THE WORLD

When I was in fifth grade, we went to Reno, Nevada for a whole year, gassed up the VW van and hit the highway. If we had to pee, my dad wouldn't even stop.

"I gotta go."

"Number one or number two?"

"Y'know." I'd pinch myself. "I gotta urinate."

"Awright." He'd downshift and swerve over into the gravel. I'd slide open the side door, and one of my brothers would grab the back of my belt so I wouldn't fall out. As we motored along, I'd whip out my wang and whiz right out the door, spraying my other brothers in the back seats.

"HEY, YOU'RE PEEIN' ON US."

"Big deal." There was a reason we'd call dibs on the shotgun seat.

We drove all across the United States of America, stopped to see the Rocky Mountains and Pike's Peak and did some other junk and made it to Reno, Nevada, the biggest little city in the world. It was about the same size as Kalamazoo, but it was tons different. It was a weird year.

The year before, I'd raised a 4H leader dog for the blind, raised it from a puppy, and I'd never been so sad as that day I had to give him away. I was supposed to be happy to help out the blind, but I wasn't, I loved that dog a lot, and I was so glad when we showed up at the house in Reno and there was a white German shepherd there. His name was Coyota.

He belonged to the people who lived at the house where we were staying, but the fat neighbor guy that always wore Hawaiian shirts, he was supposed to be watching and taking care of that dog. But he had a foxy girlfriend that was too young and good looking for him and he didn't care about the dog that much, and our house was the dog's real home, Coyota liked it there, and I liked having him around, made him my dog, spent most of my free time taking him for walks in the desert.

Every day after school, we'd head for the hills, exploring mine shafts and having a blast. I'd take a break and play with scorpions, pull the tails off lizards. And once we discovered a ghost town out in the middle of nowhere, and another time we found an oasis, a tiny forest in the middle of the desert, with owls swooping down from the trees, and a porcupine too. My dog thought he'd found a snack, and I had to pluck those quills from his cold nose. I felt bad but I had to do it.

That dog was the coolest dog in the whole wide world, if you want to know the truth. I can't stop thinking about him. The people who owned the house where we were staying never knew where Coyota had lived before he came there. The dog had just jumped through the window one summer night, with a bullet in his side. He sat down in the living room. The wound healed and he stayed. And then we moved there, a few years later. When I'd take him for a walk and he'd hear a gunshot, he'd always take off like a bullet. He might have been part coyote, that's what people said and I believed it. He didn't like to be chained up.

When we'd take off in the VW van, he'd run alongside and jump in the shotgun window if it was opened, and after we learned to roll it up, he'd follow us down the dirt road, into the four-lane highway. I'd look out the back window, clock him at 40 mph, watch him trying to keep up with us, cars passing him. He was something else. That's what he was. And we had horses too, two of them, it was like living in the country but out in the desert, at the end of Hoge Road.

One of the horses always tried to jump the fence, always got his legs wrapped up in the barbed wire. He was a stallion, I bet that's what he was, and the other horse was a girl horse, had a big round belly. One day the colt came out, wobbled around on its long legs. It was so cute. I hate to say that word, but that's what it was. And the same day that baby horse was born, Coyota caught an alien, a real alien, he killed it and was dragging it around. "IT'S AN ALIEN. From outer space."

"No, it's not," my dad told me. "It's the placenta."

"What's that?"

"The afterbirth. From the horse."

"Oh." I didn't know what that meant, it looked like an alien to me, and we had a big cat named Big White Kitty. He only had one eye. That stallion had kicked out the other one from his head. And in the stable, there was a saddlebag hanging on a nail, a nest of little baby birds inside the sack. I already said that word once so I'm not going to say it again, but I'd check on the birds every day after school, listen to them chirp, watch them open their beaks waiting for a worm or something. It was pretty cool, but one day I spotted a big-fat snake crawling along the rim of the saddlebag. I was hoping I'd got there just in time, but that snake had three lumps in its belly, and I looked in the bag and knew what those lumps had to be. I took a shovel and bashed in the head of that snake, chopped him up with the edge of the shovel and tried to free those little birds, but it was too late, the birds were dead. I was really mad about that, for a long time. I'm still mad about that.

And the kids in Reno were pretty weird too, had parents that worked in the casinos, that weren't home at night. I'd never seen that before. And most of the kids were from broken families.

I couldn't even understand that, had never met a stepparent before moving there, didn't even know what that meant. Back then it wasn't easy to get a divorce, you had to have a good reason to tell the judge before you do that, and you had to get permission from your church. But it was different in Reno. It was a cinch to get a divorce there, the easiest place in America. They had drive-up marriage booths across the street from drive-up divorces. It was simple as getting your snapshots developed at the Fotomat. I'd never seen anything like it.

It's probably like that all over now, and that's something to think about because it wasn't good, not for me at least. Of course, some of it was just being the new kid in town, a kid that talked funny and had long hair. I was a target for bullies, and a new friend for kids who didn't have any.

My best friend was from the trailer park, and he tricked me into peeing on an electric fence, thought that was funny but it wasn't. Another time, he tried to drown me in pink liquid soap, just for the heck of it, and this other bully from the trailer park caught me walking home one night, stole my Charleston Chew and tried to make me give him a piggyback ride across the desert. He was twice my size, and it was awful trying to carry him, almost worse than drowning in liquid soap. I had to drop his head on a rock and run home. I didn't even care if his skull had maybe cracked open and blood had spurted out of his head and he died out there in the desert because he'd made me really mad and I didn't want to see him again. Of course he lived, and after that, I had to avoid him and get off the school bus at the apartments miles away and walk home through the desert.

It was at those apartments I met a kid named Kirk Strange. He had a monster cartoon poster in his room that said, *As I walk through the valley of the shadow of death, I fear no evil because I'm the meanest son of a bitch in the whole valley.* He had a cuss word right on his wall, and he was a real friend, never tried to drown me in liquid soap or nothing, and once at the bus stop that bully that had tried to make me give him a piggyback ride across the desert started messing with me, and Kirk Strange got right in his face and told him to leave me alone. That was a good lesson because Kirk was no bigger than me, and that big bully backed down. That made me think about the reason and I decided that I'd never let anybody pick on me again. That was something good in all the bad.

Meanwhile, my older brothers were having the times of their lives in Reno, running around pellmell, riding dirt bikes and shooting me with pellet guns. And mauling with girls.

"I've had two furs in one day," my brother Mike told me once. Then he looked at his Timex. "And it's not even five o'clock."

"Cool." I didn't know what the heck he was talking about, but he sure looked happy. I was happy for him too, but for me there was only one fur I cared about and her name was Janene Barger. She had to wear those braces that went like barbed wire across her face, and I still remember how her voice sounded, kind of gravelly, but soft too. She was always a little sad, and I understood how she felt and I knew if we got together everything would be good again. I'd loved girls before, but there was something different about how I felt about Janene Barger. I was born just so I could meet her, that was the main reason. That's what I figured. She was the one for me, the reason I'd gone to Reno, the reason to go on living. My brothers had told me that Nevada chicks were a cinch, you just have to go for it, and I was planning on doing just that. I just had to wait for the right moment. In the meantime, I played strip poker with the girl with cooties.

Her name was Missy McDaniels. She was really dirty, like a girl version of Pigpen from the Peanuts, came to the bus stop all filthy, with elastic slacks with holes in them so you could see her underwear, and she didn't even wear shoes, not even to school. I'd never seen that before.

Of course, I'd been to church in bare feet, when we were traveling or when it was hot in the summer, so I knew that shoes and socks weren't that important, could kind of relate with Dirty Missy and her messy ways. She was something else, the definition of dirt-poor. She wrote the book on that subject. She lived with her fat mom and skinny step-dad and her weird brother. They lived in this shack that wasn't even like a house. It was behind the trailer park, out in the desert without even a driveway or a garage. But she was really nice to me because I was new in town and everybody else was mean to her. She was actually kind of cute, if she would have just washed her face, and one day she asked me if I wanted to go to her house after school. I nodded and I went.

Her brother Tommy was so glad because he didn't have any friends, but I didn't want to talk to him because he tried too hard to get your attention and people had told me that he'd done things with his Saint Bernard-like dog. It's the kind of junk that is too weird to even tell you about.

They didn't have any food in the house so me and Missy had to dig turnips from the backyard, and I felt kind of bad for her and as long as nobody was watching, I liked being nice to her. It was almost like I had a crush on her. She was really friendly with me, and even though my heart belonged to Janene Barger, I felt happy to be with a girl. We decided to play strip poker.

I had never done that before so we went in her shed, sat down Indian-style on an old mattress and started playing cards, five-card draw with pieces of clothes for betting. It was pretty scary but tons of fun too, I have to admit that. She didn't care about losing. In fact, I think she was cheating so she could get naked. She had a dirty face but the rest of her was pretty clean. Her skin had tons of freckles. I had a huge boner, and she thought that was funny. She seemed happy to see that.

I had a feeling something was going to happen and I wouldn't have to do much to make it happen. She was getting really frisky and touching my boner and it felt really good. I figured it would be good practice so I'd know what to do with Janene Barger, but actually I had forgotten all about Janene, was feeling like maybe this was okay. Even though people teased her, they didn't have to know, and they hadn't seen her all happy and clean and naked too. I was pretty happy.

But her brother Tommy busted in with his big drooling dog and ruined everything. Missy thought it was funny, didn't seem to care, but I did. He'd done things with that dog and it was time for me to put on my pants and get out of there. It was time for supper. I had to go. I went home.

And of course, her brother told everybody at school the next day, told everybody about everything, and I saw Janene Barger's face when she heard him. I knew right then that it wasn't just me, that she had liked me too or that she at least knew I liked her but I figured after she heard that, that ruined my plans and I wanted to go back in time so I'd still have a chance with her, so I could get her a mood ring and she could be my girlfriend, but it was too late for all that.

And I had to go to school with Janene Barger for the rest of the year. She was always right there at the front of my classroom, always knowing that I'd gotten naked with the girl with cooties. I felt really bad, like socking Tommy right in his big mouth. I'm still mad at him, and still mad at myself, not just for blowing it with Janene Barger, but also because I never talked to Missy again. I blamed her for messing junk up with me and Janene, but it wasn't her fault. I realize that now.

COLORFUL COLORADO

My mom was a housewife, like most moms, and she had gone to college and became an Avon lady because it was time for women's lib, and my dad was super smart, and he was super strong too, could probably whoop your dad's ass without even trying, even with one hand tied behind his back, but for some reason he wasn't interested in getting in fist-fights. Instead he went back to school when he already had a bunch of kids, and he was teaching classes and he had summers off so we'd go on tons of trips, down to Kentucky or out West, living on back-seat lunches of dry boloney sandwiches and jugs of Wyler's, cans of beef stew warmed over a campfire, that was the best, camping for weeks, spelunking in caves, drinking out of creeks, climbing mountains, heading off the trail and finding ghost towns where nobody had been for decades, hiking into canyons.

One time we went to Colorado, stayed in Aspen for a whole month. It was when Nixon quit, and I must have been about nine years old, just finished third grade, and Dad disappeared into the Rockies for weeks while we rented a place at the edge of town, at the base of the mountain. It was a ski lodge but during the summer it was cheap, about sixty bucks for the thirty days. We'd always gone tent-camping on our trips so this was a big deal. It was before Aspen turned into a place for dipshits and twits, movie stars and filthy-rich idiots. When we were there, it was just a small town, mostly just John Denver and a bunch of ski-bums and hippies. Mr. Denver didn't even come to town, and the town didn't even have streetlights. Instead, it just had torches along the roads.

I met this kid there, and I don't remember his name, but we became best friends for that whole month. He was from Chicago and told lots of fibs about getting in street fights and junk. (He was really a Jewish kid from the suburbs but I didn't figure that out until years later.) We showed off our scars and he had a big wormy appendix one on his belly from a switchblade battle and we'd have jackknife sword fights at the park and the hippies would say that ain't even cool, violence ain't the answer, give peace a chance and all that. They were pretty cool, chucked the Frisbee to us, but we thought they were dipshits when they said that. That didn't even make sense to us.

We had a blast that month, climbing to the tippy-top of Aspen Mountain and going in mine shafts and junk, even found these nudist apartments. We'd crawl up by the chair-lift and watch those crazy people, especially this one lady sitting butt-naked on the diving board with her legs spread apart and her big thing showing. She was a loudmouthed booze-hound, always spilling her bottle all over herself, chugging on a gallon jug of Gallo wine. We'd watch her for hours.

Sometimes my new best friend's little sister would try to tag along, Cherry Leibowitz was her name, not that I really cared. She was a grade below me, tons younger, almost a whole year but she did some arithmetic and figured out we'd be the same age later in the year, but I was nine and a half right then and didn't want to talk to her. She was cute, everybody could see that, but I didn't care and for some reason she decided to fall in love with me. She'd even tell me that, grab the straps of my tank top and look up at me and say that sentence right to my face. My sister thought that was so cute, but it wasn't. That girl didn't even say my name right, was always chewing Chiclets and had teeth missing and didn't talk right. She'd follow me around like that red balloon in that movie from France. And one day I went to the pool and my brothers jumped me, made me get married to her. My sister was part of it too, like the maid of honor. Cherry even had two rings, tabs from pop cans, and I tried to get away but my brother twisted my arm until I said *UNCLE*.

"Say yes."

"YES."

"Say YES, I DO."

"YOU'RE BREAKIN' MY ARM."

"SAY IT."

"Okay." They made me say it. "Yes, I do."

"You may now kiss the bride."

"Not even." Cherry puckered up, but I sure wasn't about to kiss her. I told her to get lost and then her big eyes filled with big tears, because I hurt her feelings or something. That didn't make me feel good, but I didn't really care. If you think about it, it was her fault in the first place.

After that, she seemed to give up on me and I was glad, for the most part. I had other junk to do. Me and my friend made big plans for the last night before he went back home, were going to sneak out at night and do a bunch of rotten stuff, crowbar open the Pepsi machine and swipe all the pop and nickels, and then open this window and snab the wine bottle sitting on the window sill, and bust the glass in the swimming pool and make the water turn red. I was serious as a heart attack, figured he was too. But he started making up lame excuses why we shouldn't do the wine part, because he once knew this kid that had done that and they'd made him empty the whole pool with a spoon.

"With a spoon?"

"It's true. I heard that."

"Uh-huh." He was lying, right to my face.

"I don't think we should do that."

"Awright." But I figured at least we'd get the pop machine, so I snuck out my window that night. I planned on talking him into doing it all, figured after we got the pop, he'd go for the rest, and even just the machine would be pretty cool, something to tell all my friends back home.

So I went to the pool where we were supposed to meet but he wasn't there. After waiting awhile, I headed over to the window of his bedroom and tapped on it, but nothing happened, so I tapped again and again, was about to get super mad when the window slid open. But it was Cherry.

"Where's your brother?"

"He's sleeping on the davenport."

"Go get him."

"Okay." So she climbed down and went to get him, but she came back alone. "He says that he's sick. He can't come out tonight."

"What?" This was our last chance to do all that junk.

"What were you guys going to do?"

"Nothin'." I walked off and went back to the pool, sat down against the fence, was really mad at him. He was probably going to tell his friends in Chicago that he did do it, and that's all that mattered to him, but not to me, that's why you don't make up stories because then you don't have to do junk to brag about. Bragging is important but not as important as doing it.

Then I saw someone coming, figured it was him, that he was going to at least come see me. Even if he was too sick to do all that fun junk, he'd still come out and we could go watch the nude people or something. But it wasn't even him.

"Is your brother comin'?"

"He's sick."

"Yeah right." Likely story.

"What were you guys going to do?"

"Stuff."

"What stuff?"

"Stuff you don't need to know about."

"Are you going to do it without him?"

"Prob'bly not." It ain't no fun doing it by yourself.

"I could help you."

"Not even." It wasn't stuff that girls do. "You're wearin' pj's." Or a nightgown, whatever you call it. "And slippers."

"I could go change."

"It ain't for girls."

"What is it?"

"It's none of your business." But she really wanted to know so I told her the whole plan, breaking into the pop machine and stealing the wine, everything we'd planned to do.

"I can't do that."

"I told you." I knew it wasn't for girls.

"You still have your ring?"

"Fat chance." I certainly wasn't carrying it around with me.

"I always have mine."

"Goody-goody gumdrops for you."

"I'll keep it forever."

"So what?" She kept it on a chain around her neck. "What do that proof?"

"What DOES that PROVE."

"That's what I'm axin' you. What do it proof?"

"It's proof that I'm married."

"Not even."

"I'm Cherry Winch."

"What?" That don't sound right.

"That's my name."

"My foot." If that's her name, my name must be mud.

"Where are you going?"

"Beats me." I walked away, but of course she tagged along.

"Wait up."

"How come y'always tailin' me?"

"You don't want me to?"

"It's a free country." So she followed me up by the chair-lift. I told her she had to get on her belly and do a GI Joe crawl up through the aspen trees, and of course she was a girl and didn't want to do that, but she had no choice, if she wanted to see this, she had to do that. "Look."

"Oh my gosh. They're naked."

"No duh, Sherlock." There were only a few of them because it was late at night, but you could see them really good because the lights were on. You could see everything.

"I can't look."

"Suit yourself." But I felt kind of weird, because she wouldn't. And to tell the truth, I ended up letting her kiss me, if that's what she wanted to do. "You can't tell your brother."

"Okay."

"You swear?"

"Swear to God."

"Awright." I don't know why it mattered, I was never going to see him again, and he was a liar anyway and kissing her wasn't like all that bad junk we'd planned to do but it was better than doing nothing. After we wet-kissed for a while, we took a break to catch our breaths, and she snuggled into my chest and we watched the shooting stars and listened to the aspen trees make those noises.

"I love that sound."

"Big deal."

"Aspen trees are the biggest living things in the whole wide world."

"Not even. They're just dinky trees."

"I read that."

"That don't make no sense."

"I still love how they sound." And of course, she had to look at me and say that stupid sentence about how she felt about me again.

"Why you always say that?"

"Because it's true."

"Who cares." Girls make a big deal out of almost nothing.

"Wanna kiss me again?"

"I guess." There wasn't much else to do.

PART THREE:
BACK HOME

All School Wrestling

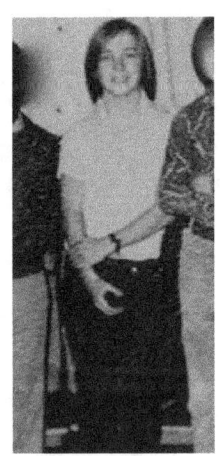

Lou

Winch
("Wrestle This")

FIRST CONFESSION

I told you some about Reno, Nevada, but I'll tell you some more. It wasn't all rotten like maybe I made it sound, we could sneak coins in the slot machines at the filling stations, at everywhere, and I learned to ski that year, up by Lake Tahoe. We had ski areas in Michigan, one that was built on a landfill, a whole hill of garbage, so they covered it with dirt and made a ski area out of it, but I'd never gone skiing before, not when Snurfing was free, but by Reno there was one ski area that was just for ski school, lessons all morning, recess all afternoon, nobody allowed there but school-age kids going to the ski school, so just a bunch of Reno riffraff, a free bus up there, every weekend.

It wasn't the best ski area around Tahoe, not like Squaw Valley or something, more low-rent, crazy cheap, about twenty bucks for the whole year so my parents bunched together my Christmas and my birthday and got me and some of my brothers secondhand skis, mine red, white and blue, ski poles and boots and everything, and the annual pass at that ski area. I had never gotten a present like that, usually got jipped when they'd combine the gifts, but that year I made out like a guy with a Siamese wife, had a blast every weekend, just rope-tows and T-bars, no chair-lifts but who cares.

After we were done skiing, my parents would pick us up where the bus dropped us off, and we'd have to go to church, that was part of the deal, so there we were, the whole Winch clan making a racket as we walked into that church, still sporting our secondhand ski boots and orange Frostline home-sewn down coats, stinky and sweaty, mop-tops matted and messy, our heads looking like a bunch of little Rod Stewart heads when we'd pocket the hats, everyone staring at us as we stomped into that church, like I said, making a lot of noise, walking up to get Communion.

I was used to people staring at us, that's just what people did when the Winch clan walked by, but I had to have my first confession at that church. I will never forget that, showed up early that night, walked into the booth and spilled my guts through that barred window.

It was kind of like a rock group's first album, back when they were just getting started and had a decade of junk to shout about, not like later ones when they only had a matter of months to come up with stuff. The next time I confessed, I wouldn't have that much material, but for my first session, I had tons to talk about, figured I'd better cough up the facts and spit them all out. I sung my songs, told my tales, just rambled on and on until the priest said that's enough for today, maybe come back next month, say some Our Fathers and Hail Marys, quit swiping coins from the collection basket.

So I said cool, Father, Son and the Holy Ghost, walked out of that booth feeling pretty good. I liked being Catholic, being forgiven, doing the sins and saying amen, making amends, I had no problem with that. I stomped my ski boots across the floor, over to where my family was sitting. I could tell people were whispering and peeking at me, but like I said, I was used to that. It was before Mass, but a few dozen people were already there by the time I'd gotten done confessing, and when I sat down next to my brother Bob, he was busting a gut.

"What's so funny?"

"You were talkin' so loud."

"You could hear me confessin'?"

"Everybody could hear you."

"Oh." Bummer.

FAMILY PICNIC

While we were living in Reno, we took a trip to Yosemite National Park, mostly avoided the valley because that's where everybody went and my dad didn't like that, took us to the high country, taught us how to rock climb and rappel down the cliffs. That was great, but my favorite day was when my mom took me and my little brothers up the mountain to have a family picnic.

They were up ahead on the path and I was diddle-daddling around behind them, just enjoying being by myself and checking out the views, whittling a stick and peeing on trees.

Meanwhile, my mom thought someone was coming down the path toward them, but it turned out to be a big bear. She grabbed my little brothers and headed into the woods, figured the bear would probably eat me but did the arithmetic and figured it was better to save as many kids as she could.

After the bear passed them, she thought about running down the path to warn me but still decided it was better to stay with my little brothers, to save them and only lose one kid.

My brothers say it was just a matter of numbers, could have been any of us, but I like to think it was one of those good things about being a middle kid, being left alone to take care of myself.

I could have been like Daniel Boone, or Davy Crockett, whichever one wrestled a bear, I'd be like him if I did that, have a good story to tell. And if the bear ate me, that would be a good story too, but probably my mom would have felt bad. She still felt bad but I told her that's okay, I liked that adventure. That bear caught me off guard, came around the corner like he owned that forest, didn't care about sharing the trail. He outweighed me a lot but I figured it would be a fair fight because I had my jackknife and a good point going on that stick. That's probably why he decided not to wrestle or even mess with me, but if he had, I'd be okay with that. That was still cool.

INTENSIVE CARE

When we were almost done with Nevada, the people came back to the house where we were staying, so we got a little cabin up by Lake Tahoe, just a few backyards from the water, with a big screen door and wooden floors. It was cool up there, the water in the lake clean and deep, the crayfish big as lobsters, and they were filming *The Godfather Part II* down the street, so it was bomb, people walking around dressed up like mobsters, like they were living in the past. They tried to pay my dad a bunch of money to be in that movie but he wasn't interested. He already looked like he lived in the past without even trying, but he thought being in a movie would be boring. I understood that because why pretend to have fun when you can do real stuff instead. That's what we did, climbed up cliffs and cannonballed in the water, dove off the dock and caught crawdaddies.

Before we headed back to Michigan, my big brother Mike went down to Reno to see his best-friend Daryl, for one last time. My folks weren't too thrilled about that because the pair had gotten in a lot of trouble that year, ran away to Texas, got thrown in jail. Of course, my mom and dad probably figured what could happen in one day. But Mike and Daryl went dirt-biking that night.

I remember waking up and realizing something was wrong. I was used to seeing my brothers get hurt and going to the emergency room, but this was all dark and confusing and everybody was too worried about Mike to care about what I was thinking. My dad went to the hospital.

The next day I found out the deal, Mike and Daryl had been dirt-biking on one bike, booking down Hoge Road without lights or helmets, Daryl driving, my brother on back. A guy in a car didn't see them, swerved in front of them. The bike slammed into the side of the car, catapulted Mike off the back, sent him sailing. About fifty yards down the road, a boulder finally stopped him, pulverized his pelvis, snapped his spine, shattered his ribs. The bones punctured his lung, stabbed his kidney. He was hurt really bad, worse than anything I'd heard of. It didn't look good for him.

When I finally went to see him, his room reeked like something awful that I didn't want to think about and he wasn't awake, didn't look like my brother at all, had wounds all over and tubes going everywhere. I didn't like seeing him like that, didn't want to think it but I knew the odds were against him. I hate to say that, but that's the way it seemed to me. He was probably going to die.

BACK TO THE ZOO

While Mike was in intensive care for about a month, most of the rest of us moved back to Kalamazoo. Mike was still in the hospital but finally got good enough to travel on a plane and came home. Doctors tried to tell him that he'd never walk again, but he told them he was a Winch, would end up dancing on their graves, so he had to live up to that bragging, put that holy water on his wounds, and after a few seasons and a lot of screaming and cramps and painkillers, he was back on his feet, back in the game, walking with crutches but shooting hoops and everything, playing kick-the-can instead of kicking the bucket. I sure was happy about that, didn't think that liquid was going to work because it just tasted like regular water to me, but he was getting better all the time.

Before too long, he chucked the crutches and got himself a cane, tapping the blacktop and smacking the tennis ball, swaggering the streets like a gangster, got off the oatmeal and applesauce and started greazing solid food, grubbing on foot-long Galley subs and crunching on bags of Jay's potato chips, chomping on Screaming Yellow Zonkers and chasing the girls, showing off his scars and having a blast. He still had a limp but he was alive, that's the important thing.

And he sued that guy in the car so he was probably the first filthy-rich Winch in the history of the human race. In a year or two he'd be dirt poor again, but in the meantime he scored himself a Cutlass, used to order extra-large pizza pies all the time, back when they'd probably just invented delivery, Domino's Pizza, back when it was mostly just local and good and greasy, started by some dirt-poor Michigan orphan who'd end up getting carried away and going a little crazy, buying tons of stuff, even the Detroit Tigers. But back then, that pizza was the best, if you can believe that, and the rest of us would gather around and watch Mike filling his pimpled face, slurping on double-syrup Cokes, greazing on double-cheese pizza, telling us that he'd give us a slice if he didn't get stuffed. So we'd wait and watch, wishing and sniffing, drooling and hoping. Of course, we should have known better. He was a Winch, never got full.

It wasn't long before everyone else gave up, went outside to play ditch 'em, but I stuck around, thought maybe he'd show me some mercy because he'd chopped off my thumb that one time, certainly didn't want to blow my chance, figured without everyone else, I had a better chance to get a whole slice to myself, maybe at least a piece of that crust. I never even got that, but that's the way it goes, he'd more than paid the price to be greedy like that. I'm not mad about that, barely even remember it. It was his pizza. So he ate it. That was the Winch way anyway.

And there's more than one way to get a slice of pizza. In fact, I could tell you tons of ways to do that. Just for example, you could go down to Tony's Pizza and play some pinball, put the phonebooks under the legs and rack up some free games on Captain Fantastic, kill some time and rogue the leftovers. People left half-eaten slices on their plates. I could never understand that. Nobody had to tell me about starving people in Africa. I had a belly myself, liked to pat it and feel something. And Mike wasn't always selfish with his wealth, probably still felt bad about being greedy with the goulash, used to send money to those people in Africa, used to fly down to Cleveland to see a ball game, leave the car keys in his bedroom. That seemed like an invite.

I'd grab the *Yellow Pages* and look through the white section, do it by the book and let my fingers do the walking, rip out the address and slide the book under my butt so I could see out the windshield, turn the key and fire up the engine, go see Tammi Lee, tell her to grab the bikini.

"I'm still in my pj's."

"Yep." I could see that.

"You got wheels?"

"Cutlass Supreme."

"I'll go change."

"Cool." You can't steal a girl's love, but you can steal your brother's car. You can't buy love, but you can buy tickets to the water slide. After that, I didn't care too much about Mike eating all the pizza pie. He deserved all that, wiped his face on his sleeve, took a flight to Cleveland and enjoyed America's favorite pastime, greazing on hot dogs. While he did that, I was doing something else, joyriding and picking up girls, going to the water park. He'd already done all that, but now he was settling down. He'd learned his lesson, but I hadn't done that yet.

SHAG CARPETING

When we moved back to Kalamazoo, we had to get a new place to stay, not just another rental, my dad bought a house, on the same street but a few blocks over. We'd owned a home once before, but that house is barely a memory, more a slide in the projector than an image in my head, just stories I'd heard. My dad got that first one when he went back to college, bought it flat out with his scholarship money, five thousand bucks. It probably wasn't much for a family of eight, but it did the job while my dad finished school. When the well went dry, he'd bring home buckets of water. My mom would heat them on the stove so we could boil potatoes and wash our hands. She tries to tell me that I was a miserable preschooler back then, always had asthma attacks, constant trips to the emergency room. But I still think I had good times there, the snow deep in the winter, patches huge on my knees. I'd put bread bags on my feet, buckle my boots and go outside.

Anyway, I know the house we bought in Kalamazoo was cool, ancient and huge, over a hundred years old. And for the first time in my life, I had my own bedroom, burlap on the walls. We were fixing the place up, so I tore down the burlap, had an asthma attack and found pink brick wallpaper under the fabric. That didn't look any better so I inhaled on my inhaler and spit up some goobers, nailed up some paneling, dark wood, simulated oak. Then I put up the decorations, O. J. Simpson and Mario Andretti, Bobby Orr and pictures of skulls and black-light posters.

My little brothers still had to share a room, but they were younger so that's what they got. They had nothing to complain about, had been saved from being eaten alive by a bear, and they had bunk beds that my dad had built and painted them orange. He made all the furniture for that place and we had it made in the shade, wall-to-wall shag like a regular house, a Ping-Pong table in the basement and a tire swing in the backyard. Our last backyard was the best one in the universe, but we had to share it with about twenty other families. Now we had a real backyard that was just our own, a place for my dad to keep all his wood. He even made some kind of device so the fireplace could heat the whole house, built a picnic table for the kitchen too, the tabletop about fifty feet long so I had some elbowroom to eat my greaze, didn't have to listen to my brothers crunching in my ears.

My sister had maybe always shared a room with my little brothers, but now she had her own room too, pictures of koala bears and all that junk on her walls, Decopodge collages of teenybopper boys and a poster of the A-bomb going off and the word *WHY?* underneath it. It was right across the hall from my room and lots of my friends thought she was a fox, would hang around the house to look at her, so I'd have to sock them a lot for saying junk. She was just a girl, but she was my only sister so I had to stand up for her, used to hang out with her when I was younger, making Easy-Bake Oven cakes and junk, even almost joined her good-guys club, but I had to tell her that I had to be in the bad-guys club because I was a boy, felt a little bad but had to do that.

When we got that new house, my sister was in junior high, her belly getting bigger all the time. Most girls got knocked up once or twice in those days, but usually they just got abortions. My sister didn't want to do that, and since the guy who got her pregnant was black, sometimes people would say stupid stuff, so I'd have to stand up for her, get in fights. She deserved my help because she was actually being brave, a flat-out bad-ass about it. And other people should mind their own businesses, thought they were just being normal and prejudiced but really they were mostly just jealous because she hadn't gone out with them. That's what I think, and I think I'm right.

Of course, that's her business, she can tell you more about that if she wants to do that. I just wanted you to see that things were changing, the living room getting rearranged to fit the situation, the upholstery going through some alterations to complement the occasion. It wasn't just that the Slick Bricks on the fireplace had to match the turd-brown color of the shag carpeting. We were living in a new house with lots of junk going on, trying to fit in back in Kalamazoo after we'd spent that year in Reno. That trip was like going to the kitchen for a snack during the break for station identification. When you came back, you had to adjust the lines on the Motorola.

It was probably harder for my sister and my older brothers, maybe even tougher for my folks dealing with junk, but mostly it was good to be back, and most people were cool, about my sister and my brother getting hurt, people like Harley's big brother Jake and all them, they were always thoughtful and bomb about junk. That always helps out, helps you roll with the punches.

When you're just trying to watch some reruns and trouble comes knocking, kicks you in the pecker when you answer the door, it's time to call your neighbors. With a little help, you can take care of old man trouble, whoop his ass, slug him where it hurts, send him home to put an ice pack on his wounds. While he's busy doing that, you can get back to your after-school snack, finish watching *The Brady Bunch*, go outside and find some fun. He's no fun to have around anyway.

And I was doing fairly cherry, just fine in my book, turned twelve that year so junk was looking up. I finally got to sink my meat-hooks into those twelve-year-old snacks. Before that, you had to load up your plate at supper or go to bed with an empty belly, but after you waved your hand over a dozen candles, you blew out the flames and your wish came true. I finally got to put those twelve-year-old molars to good use, got edibles most every night, chomping on a bowl of King Vitamin at the oversized picnic table, filling my belly and busting a gut, laughing at my little brothers.

Their times would come, but mine had arrived like a ring at the door, a man on the other side with a smile on his face and a double-cheese pizza in his hands. I never got nothing like that, but you get my drift. I was doing all right with myself. I was still the shortest kid in my class, but so was Napoleon Bonaparte and he crowned himself king, almost conquered the whole wide world. I was growing up like a mug, felt like the crowned King of Kalamazoo, or at least the king of the King Vitamin, king of the Winch kitchen for a night, I know that, that's something, something to brag about. I had a backyard and a bedroom of my own, black lights shining on my pirate-ship poster, fish net on my ceiling, Penthouse Pets to keep me company, a couple of eight-tracks for my dime-store deck, snacks in the evening. I had it made in the shade, nothing to complain about.

JACKKNIVES

Now that I think about it, we had a pretty kick and killer place to grow up. But I was still just a kid, mostly just thinking about myself or not thinking much at all, back at West Main Elementary for one last year, sixth grade on the second floor, just doodling on my desk and looking out the window, watching the people at Harding's Friendly Market. Next to that, housewives were washing their dirty girdles at Norge Village, smoking Virginia Slims and gossiping, sipping on cans of Fresca and folding their sheets right out in the parking lot. After recess, the afternoon dragged on like long division. The Norge globe spun around like the hand on the clock, but before the bell rang, I got to get out of class, tightened the orange belt around my waist, the strap over my shoulder. I was a safety, like the fuzz of West Main School, told those kindergarten babies they better stop, look, and listen, wait till I say the coast is clear, hanging out with Rick Poling after school.

Ricky was my best friend and like best friends do, he was waiting for me when I got back from Reno. For years, I'd been going to his house for school lunch, eating peanut butter and honey sandwiches and watching Yogi Bear cartoons. He had color and cable, and his mom was always home, always nice to you, like all the moms, always around, cooking pot roasts and putting clothes on the line, so I spent that year with Ricky, chucking darts in the basement, clipping flower buds with our bullwhips, flinging Frisbees and boomerangs. Mostly, we played with our jackknives.

They hadn't invented Asteroids, Pac Man or anything like that yet, and there were only so many reruns to watch, so we'd play mumblety-peg or root-the-peg, carve two twigs into pegs, take turns chucking our knives in the ground, flicking the tip off your thumb and on to the next round, off your shoulder or elbow, your nose or whatever, whatever positions you decided before the game started. If you got the blade to stick in the dirt, if you did and he didn't, you'd get one pound on his peg, use the butt of your knife to knock it in the ground. When one person made it through all the moves, the game was over, and the loser had to dig his peg from the ground with his front teeth, even if it was buried, biting at the ground like Mike Mulligan's steam shovel, spitting out the

89

dirt and going back for the peg. It wasn't fun losing, but those were the rules.

With the other game, you'd stand face to face, spread your legs and grab your balls, chuck the knife between your friend's feet. If it stuck, he had to move one of his sneakers to the blade. You'd take turns until the space between your feet was the length of your knife, then you lost and we'd play again, after school, all year long until the ground froze, bare feet in the summertime.

One time, I stuck the knife in Rick's foot and another time he got me in the belly, but that's just what happens if you play with knives. And if you think about it, it's worth it. It was something to do instead of doing nothing. It was fun, that's what it was.

Sometimes after school or on Saturday after cartoons, Punk Taylor and Rod Ovens would come over to play with us. Punk always had a sharp blade because he lived at a house attached to a lawnmower repair shop, Taylor's Lawnmowers by Duffy's Miniature Golf, but Ovens on the other hand, he didn't have a blade to his name so one time, it was a warm tornado-weather Saturday afternoon that day, and Ovens showed up with his transistor radio instead of a knife, wanted us to dance in the driveway, to make up skits to go with the AM station top-forty tunes. We'd each get a turn, make a game out of it, see who could do better. That was his bright idea, and I looked at Punk and Rick and I knew they were thinking the same thing as me. We didn't know what to say, it was like Rod Ovens had just told us he wanted to kiss us on the lips or something. We ditched him right then and there, took off down the road telling the whole wide world what we'd just found out.

"ROD OVENS IS A HOMO."

"HE'S A FAG."

"FOR DAYS."

"FOR SURE." We knew that for a fact.

Of course the next year, Rod would get Karen Kamnikar as a girlfriend, the best-looking fur of a girl in the whole seventh grade, the one I really liked, and I know what Rod Ovens was thinking then. He was thinking, *Who's the fag now, Winch?* That's what he was thinking. I know it.

SUMMER CAMP

I went to Boy Scout camp that summer, earned the money myself, planting trees and picking up rubbish, made the money and went to camp, probably had the worst troop of the bunch, never knew what a bunch of delinquents we were until I saw the other kids. It was great, meeting up in the woods with the East Side riffraff, smoking Swishers and telling fibs, talking about fur. Some of the kids in our troop had to go to Boy Scouts, there or juvie, and we had bows and arrows, rifles and fireworks, had a good time. On visiting day, all us kids who knew our parents weren't coming had it all planned out. When the station wagons pulled up, we lit a row of bottle-rockets, watched this other kid run out of his cabin wearing nothing but his sneakers, streaking across the line of parents.

The moms and dads got back in their cars and headed home, glad to get rid of their rotten kids for a few weeks. That was great, something to laugh about over the campfire, cooking hot dogs on sticks, greazing marshmallows and chucking Black Cats on the flames, sneaking out at night. I was younger, mostly just watched, but I was a Winch. When they handed me the joint, I took it.

That was the first time I smoked pot, at Boy Scout camp. But it was a pin joint, and I didn't even catch a buzz. I'd smoke more in the years that followed, tons of Paraquat Mexican and mean-green homegrown, quarter pounds of Colombian gold and a few more pounds of red bud, bags of sinsemilla and ounces of hash and Thai sticks, opium and hash oil and whatever we could score.

BE PREPARED

I was pretty excited about starting seventh grade, going to Hillside Junior High, having different teachers, changing classes. I'd spent all of my life with hand-me-downs, but being twelve years old and going to a new school was a big deal, and even my mom knew that. I got a brand-new binder with sections for each class, went to Okum Brothers and scored some sweat socks and Converse irregulars, a jockstrap for PE class, gray corduroys and a rugby shirt with red and white stripes, went to Meijer's Thrifty Acres for that. That was a cool shirt back then. I had to spend my paper-route money on the Coors tank top but it was worth it. I was set, styling for seventh grade.

When we were splitting from the store, some fool in an El Camino had left his lights on, so I opened the door, pushed the knob on the dash. Of course, an eight-track was sticking out the deck, Queen *Sheer Heart Attack*, so I snabbed it, figured he owes me that for saving his battery, slipped the tape in my bag. But when I got home, my mom dumped it out. "Where'd you get this tape?"

"What?" The label was all wrinkled. "Got what?"

"This."

"Oh that." I couldn't think of much to say, figured I was busted and couldn't be trusted. But I wasn't one to admit to defeat, came up swinging. "I got that outa the used bin."

"The used bin?"

"Yeah. That's what I said." Of course, Meijer's Thrifty Acres certainly didn't have a used bin, but I figured it was worth a try. "It cost a quarter. I used my allowance."

"Meijer's has a used bin?"

"Course." It's possible. "It's in the back. You prob'bly just ain't never seen it."

"Uh-huh." She had seen me go in that car, should have figured out the deal.

"That's the deal. What I said."

"Oh." She was a pushover, not like my dad. "Okay."

"Cool." I took the tape, went upstairs and pushed it in my deck at the foot of my bed, jammed out to "Stone Cold Crazy," stripped down and decided to beat my peter looking at the nude girls in *Cosmopolitan*, the black-and-white photos in the "Cosmo Tells All" section.

"Hey." My sister knocked on my door. "You know what happened to my new *Cosmo*?"

"Who knows." I cracked the door. "Whaddya want?"

"Whaddya doin'?"

"None of your beeswax."

"You know what I read in *Cosmo*?"

"Who cares. I know I don't."

"It says that eighty percent of teenage boys masturbate."

"Big deal." How come she was even saying that word? "Get lost."

"And you know what the other twenty percent do?"

"Beats me." But I figured she knew I was part of that part. "What?"

"They tell fibs."

"So what?" I slammed the door in her face, stashed the magazine under my mattress, tried on my new threads. I was set, ready for anything. At least, that's what I thought.

HILLSIDE JUNIOR HIGH

When I got to school, I found my reputation waiting for me. My brothers had made sure everyone knew what to expect from a Winch. I showed up in gym class, my eyeballs all glassy from allergies, and the gym teacher started in on me. "Oh no, not another Winch."

"Yep." I was actually a pretty good kid up to that point, just told you about the bad stuff. Sure, I'd done some misdemeanors and other minor crimes, but just the junk everybody does, fist-fights and vandalism, filling up dime rolls with pennies to rob the savings-and-loan, shoplifting and joyriding, the occasional arson and junk like that. I liked changing the words to songs in music class, singing *Marijuana, marijuana, L-S-D, L-S-D, scientists make it, teachers take it, why can't we?* instead of that French song, got sent to the office and had to bend over, singing *Glory glory hallelujah, teacher hit me with a ruler.* I'd done my time after school, missing recess and scribbling sentences, scratching long lines down the paper for the I's and L's, but I did pretty good in school, found fifty-cent pieces in my pockets for good report cards, got gold stars on my spelling tests, earned an A+ on my report about the duckbilled platypus. I know I got that.

And I always kicked some serious butt in gym class, dashed to the fence and back without breaking a sweat, left the chicken-fat kids in the dust, climbed that rope and slapped the ceiling without even trying, almost even got that Presidential Physical Fitness Award, that T-shirt and certificate, the patch to put on my jean jacket, so what if I wasn't good at chucking junk, President Ford had pardoned Nixon, could've let me slide on the softball throw. He was from Michigan himself, could have cut me some slack. He's dead now, and I don't even care.

And Mr. Psychopath, my PE teacher in seventh grade, he was mean as a mug, had calves like giant frog legs, skin black and glossy like the mud on the bank by the sewer creek. I wasn't racist but he was an asshole, started getting on my nerves right from the get-go. He'd paddle my bony butt every chance he got, make me run the gauntlet just because I forgot my jockstrap. He just had it out for me, should have been proud of me that I could do more pull-ups than anybody else, that I could wind-sprint around the backstops like nobody's business. But he was always on my case.

"You flyin' high as a bird, ain't you Winch?"

"Huh?" I had no idea what he was talking about, but the other kids did, thought I must be stoned out of my mind. And it wasn't long before I lived up to their expectations, gave them what they wanted. I liked that a lot more than sitting at a desk anyway, listening to some jive turkey talking, and when I was with other teachers, some who were coaches, I wanted Mr. Psychopath to know that he was the one that was wrong, that actually I could do pretty good, if grownups would just stay off my case. Henson always believed in me so I did good in his class, had him for social studies and homeroom. But most of those teachers expected the worst so that's what they got.

It got me lots of attention anyway, and I liked that, getting in trouble. Hillside was all about that anyway, riots in the cafeteria, fist-fights all the time. I'd get kicked out of class with a handwritten referral, find a puddle of blood on the hallway tiles, follow the red dots to the main office, cop a lounge in the penalty box, cross my arms over my chest. Kids in the hall would knock on the window and I'd turn around and cheese at them. I felt good about being part of the problem.

Of course, my older brother Bob was going to Hillside that year, so I lived in the shadow of him but I didn't mind, there were lots of cute chicks hanging out there. If Bob were around, he could tell you all the stories and the junk he did, but he ain't around so I'll tell you some so you can know. All us Winches were crazy in our own ways, but all my other siblings are still around so they can tell their own tales. You might think I did some crazy junk, but compared to Bob, I didn't do much. He made me look like a choirboy singing in the back of church.

Of course, people didn't know him like I did, don't remember that he was just a regular kid most of his life, playing Rocket football, junk like that. They never listened to him play the clarinet, or jam on the guitar, never saw all the stuff he could have done, if he would have had the chance, just remember all the crazy junk he did at the end. That junk stands out.

Like one time, I ran into him down in the student ghetto, and he had about a hundred electric guitars, was just selling them to people who passed by. I asked him where he got all the guitars and he said he'd ripped off the shopping mall the night before, was just making some extra dough to score some weed. Another time, he broke into this house and stole all the stuff, dragged it all across the street. The next morning, they found him

95

in the park. He was sitting on a chair in front of a TV, smoking a cigarette with all the stuff he'd stolen. Everybody wondered why he'd done that, what he got out of ripping off junk that he didn't even use. I guess he just didn't give a rat's ass.

All that may seem like rotten junk, but he never got the chance to show people that his action-packed ways and bad-ass bravery would have led him to do junk that other people don't have the guts to do, if he'd had the chance to grow up and put all that to good use. He just needed a place where he could do his own thing. If he'd had the chance, he would have been famous or something, no doubt about it. If you knew him, you'd know that. That's the deal, and you best believe it. If you don't, I know what your problem might be. You might be a dumb-ass. And I might have to kick your ass. If you act like an ass, you're bound to get slapped.

And it wasn't just bad junk, that's the point, like one time, he was just walking down the hall and this super-tall black guy was coming at him. You were supposed to get out of his way, but my brother didn't like doing that so they ran into each other. The giant guy just laughed because he was about two feet taller than my brother, but he stopped laughing when my brother got on his tippy-toes and clipped him in the chin. That guy was really surprised when that happened, and I thought they'd get in a fight, but they didn't because that guy respected my brother for having the balls to do that. My brother was a little frustrated because he thought they were going to fight, but he got over that. They learned to respect each other without even getting suspended. That guy just needed to learn a lesson so my brother taught him one. That was one of the good things he did.

And another time he was just going for a hike, hoofing really fast like he always did, walking by the Gus Macker basketball contest that day. That event started in Michigan, was a big deal that they set up every year, pulled up with semi-trucks, filled up the parking lot with basketball hoops. Anybody could give it a try and we had about fifty billion Afro-Americans living in Kalamazoo and everybody knows that blacks are good at shooting hoops. That might sound like a stereotype, but we hadn't even heard of that word back then, and that's just the way it was, at least where I came from. People waited all year for that contest, trained every day so they could be really good. But Bob was just walking by, decided to try it. And he won the big prize, got his name in the paper, came home with the big trophy. I didn't even know he shot hoops.

He was just like that, had females crawling all over him, acting like groupies at the edge of the stage of a concert. Girls just loved him, all kinds of girls. Whole packs of females would follow behind him, trying to keep up because he walked really fast. I used to tag along and hang out with them, that was fun, always got called Little Winch when I got to Hillside, got mobbed and thumped on my head, just something stoners did to kids younger than them, thumping some seventh-grade skull. They'd all crowd into Stoners' Corner in the hallway, get me every time I had to go by there.

Mostly I hated it when them ninth-grade fry-brains did that, but the girls would give me hugs and tell them to leave me alone, and there were tons of them girls on our bus, way at the back where the ninth-grade stoners had dibs, good-looking chicks like Andrea Glass and all her friends, like this one girl that was chubby, just kind of fat and perfect in fact, had dusty-blonde pixie hair and powder-blue eye shadow to match her fuzzy sweater, just sat there when everyone else was getting rowdy and raising hell, jumping from one side of the bus to the other, in the winter, trying to make the bus wipe out, but that one girl just sitting still, kind of sad and quiet, a lot like me. She wasn't really a fox but I liked her a lot, probably even loved her. In fact, I loved her to death.

I was only a seventh-grader so I couldn't sit in the back, but I was a Winch so they let me sit in the seats right in front of them. I liked it there, tried to impress the ladies with my artistic abilities, graffiti on the seats with my el Marko magic marker, loved to listen to them fry-brain girls singing songs, swaying and harmonizing without even a radio going, singing "Mama Kin" and songs like that, and one day my brother and his stoner friends truth-or-dared me about that girl that I liked.

I decided to take the dare, took a whiff of my ink to give me some courage, clicked the cap on my marker and leaned over the seat, kissed that girl right on the mouth, licked my lips and tasted her lip gloss, was sure glad I did but didn't know what to do next. I should have asked my brother because I knew he knew the deal. I knew that for a fact because this one foxy fur girl had writing on her jeans that said *Bob Winch was here five times last night*, that sentence and an arrow pointing right to her poontang. So I knew he knew what to do, but I didn't want to tell him that I didn't. But at least I gave that girl some lip, and she gave me some back. It tasted like happiness.

After that, she didn't come to school, and I wondered what had happened. At the end of the week, I decided to ask. All those fry-brains had been quiet for a few days, and when I asked about that girl, they got even more quiet than before. Later, my brother told me she'd OD'ed on smack.

I wasn't sure what that meant, knew smack meant heroin, and that OD meant overdose, but I wasn't sure if that meant she had died. Fact of the matter, I still don't know because OD doesn't always mean that, and at the time, I didn't want to look dim or dense so I didn't ask, probably didn't want to know anyway, was just hoping she'd come back. But I never saw her again.

Maybe that taught me that you've got to go for it quick because the next day might be too late, but mostly it just made me feel sad. Now that I think about it, that still makes me feel that way.

But that's just the way it was back then, lots of people disappearing into thin dust or just plain kicking the bucket, mostly from doing too many drugs and from riding motorcycles and from driving drunk. And tons of kids offed themselves. That happened to lots of my brother's friends.

In the years that followed, kids would drop like dominoes, lots of them that I knew, but for the meantime, I was in seventh grade and most of the people I knew were still alive. I had a good imagination, and I imagined that girl that I liked was sitting somewhere getting the help she needed. She probably had counselors and a cozy room and was feeling better about herself and about life. I wanted to believe she was okay, so that's what I believed. It wasn't like a few years later when all that junk about people dying would get in my face and get to me a lot. I could see it was already getting to my brother, but I didn't understand until I got there myself. At the time, I was just a kid, glad to be done with elementary school, starting my life at junior high. I was pretty happy.

JOCKSTRAPS & VARSITY JACKETS

Back then, sports were free so if you wanted to be in them, you could do that. Years later, maybe people would think more about putting people in groups, like jocks do sports and maybe fry-brains don't, but it wasn't like that back then, not in junior high, not for me at least. I wasn't even a stoner yet anyway, was just getting started in seventh grade. And I wanted to do a sport.

I hated some games like baseball or any sport with small balls, wasn't really good at hitting them, or at chucking stuff, unless it was big. But I loved smear-the-queer. That was my favorite.

"That's not a school sport." That's what he told me. "Pick something else."

"I know that ain't a school sport. I'm just tellin' you what I'm good at."

"Like what?"

"What about football?"

"Football?"

"Yeah." It's kind of like smear-the-queer. "Can I play that?"

"You're kind of small."

"Big deal." I was sick of hearing that, felt like socking that fool in the face just for saying that. He obviously didn't know his history. "Ain't you ever heard of Napoleon Bonaparte?"

"How tall are you?"

"Beats me." I knew I was tall enough to clip him in the chin. Even if I couldn't reach that, I could ralph him in the belly, give him an uppercut when he bent over. "What do that matter?"

"You can't do that anyway."

"How come?"

"You have to be in eighth grade just to try out for JV."

"Oh." Bummer. "What about boxin'?"

"There's wrestling."

"Like Big Time Wrestlin'?"

"Not exactly."

"I'll still do it."

"It's not till winter."

"What can I do now?" Just give me the list.

"You can run cross-country."

"Okay, I'll do that."

"You know how to run fast?"

"Course." I knew I could run faster than that motherfucker. "Sign me up."

I knew I'd do all right, could dust cops and neighbors, only got caught once when I egged this one mug's car. And he just got lucky, caught me on a bad day. I could probably run a marathon or something, up and down a mountain, into the Grand Canyon. I dashed like nobody's business.

Of course, I didn't know cross-country meant running for a million miles.

At practice, we had to run fifteen or twenty every day, up to the mall and back again, Saturday mornings too, when I should have been eyeballing *The Banana Splits* and *Hong Kong Phooey*.

But I got used to it, and the coach was super cool, that really helped. He always ran with us, looked like a cross between Mark Spitz and the Fonz, like that guy in the Camel commercial, had a Prefontaine mustache and a really good-looking girlfriend. When he invited us over to his house for pizza, I could see she was living with him and they weren't even hitched. Mr. H. was slick, just shacking up with that foxy lady. He made comic books for his main job, ran cross-country on the side, was even best friends with the guy who made *The Archies*. He told us that and I believed it.

Before we had a meet, the older kids like Randy Parent would always outrun me, it was just the way it was, ninth-graders ran faster, but during the first meet, I busted out of the woods and realized I wasn't even tuckered out, caught my second wind and took off like a bullet, passed the pack of ninth-graders, Randy Parent and those ugly kids from that other school, passed them all and dashed up the hill to the football field, clipped that ribbon under the goal posts, never looked back.

Pretty soon, me and Maher realized that idea that ninth-graders won the race was just an obstacle to overcome, like running the four-minute mile, like that had been before someone did that, and all those eighth-graders and ninth-graders had to learn that this wasn't going to be their year, it was made for us seventh-graders, me and Maher at the front, trying to beat the clock because that was the only competition, reaching it before it clicked to twelve, racing it out to the finish line.

Sometimes, we'd let Parent win just to be respectful to our elders, but mostly it was me and Maher. Instead of being my competition, he was my seventh-grade teammate, and it didn't matter if he won or I did, it was usually one of us and that's all that mattered. The next day, they were announcing our names over the intercom, people patting me on the back, all that. That felt good.

I didn't think of it at the time, didn't think of it until right now, but that probably helped me get along, especially with the black kids. Being a brainiac was just being a smart aleck, but being an athlete meant something else. Running fast wasn't like being good at hoops, but going to junior high is like going from the top to starting over at the bottom, and it wasn't like many of us seventh-graders were sporting varsity jackets that fall. It was actually a pretty decent year to be a long-distance runner, with the jogging craze just taking off and people like Prefontaine making it hip and cool to do that. I couldn't grow a mustache like him, but I had a few hairs on my chest, plenty of pubics in my pants so I didn't feel too awkward in the showers, rubbed myself a little bit so I didn't have a shrinky-dink and could try to compete with the black guys, felt pretty slick on days of meets, hoofing down the hall sporting the meshed tank top over my Coors shirt. The black guys always slapped skin when I slipped through, patted my back and wished me luck. I was just a penniless half-pint but that made me feel like I was ten-feet tall with a million bucks in my pockets, had me looking up. Before that, I was feeling awkward and small like everyone else, with my allergy eyes and a runny nose, inhaler in my pocket and pimples on my forehead, trying to get my stupid locker open, hoping nobody noticed that my sneakers were irregulars, nodding for the reduced lunch and trying to get those pizza-bun stains from the white stripes on my new rugby shirt, hoping nobody noticed that I had a boner holding female ankles in gym class, but things were looking up, I was doing all right, just a half-witted half-pint but halfway on my way to being a bad-ass again.

BLACK CHICKS & STONER GIRLS

Like I said, there were tons of black kids in Kalamazoo, and all but maybe two or three of them lived on the North Side, so tons went to Hillside, that school was about half black, but I'd lived a few blocks from them most of my life, not that that really meant much, but I'd gone to Northglade in third grade, played with them when they got bussed to my school. I was a short kid so I'd learned the deal at a young age, wasn't prejudiced, didn't care about the color of his skin or the size of his nostrils, didn't care about his fifty cousins or if his family was on food stamps. If some bully tried to take my milk money, I'd give him a knuckle sandwich. He'd focus on some easier target.

The black chicks were pretty bad-ass, would box you in the face if they felt like it, but I never had to sweat about that, was nice to them so they liked me, and vice versa or something like that. They were nice to me because I liked them. It's the same way when dealing with anybody, a boy or a girl, an old geezer or an ugly mug, even a chink or a camel-jock. If you've ever been in a place where most of the people don't look like you, you know what it's like to have people looking at you. That makes you think about junk. You see past the pimples on a kid's face and look for other more important reasons to punch someone. Most of the time, I got in fights with other white kids.

We'd slug the crap out of each other in the middle of class, but we'd be talking to each other by the time we made it to the main office, laughing like old friends as we sat in the orange chairs.

With the black kids, I just slapped skin, five or ten, didn't have any problems. We'd lived through the first wave of bussing anyway, came up with our own versions of understanding. They knew not all white people were peckerwoods, and we knew not all black kids were niggers. We pinned most of the dumb jokes on the polacks. (It's just like years later when people would pin the dumb jokes on the blonde girls, not any better or any different.) Sure, we grew up with the words, tried to avoid nigger-rigging our engines and nigger-lipping our smokes, watched out for the nigger in the woodpile, took nigger showers if we were in a hurry, nibbled on nigger-toes at Christmastime, told the jokes and riddles, what do you call a nigger in a new house and all that, but Hillside wasn't like a shock like it had been for others before us. At least, it wasn't that way for me.

If junior high would have been the first place I had to deal with mobs of crazy black kids swaggering down the hallway, it could have been a different story. I might have studied those pamphlets my uncle was sending me, joined the Nazi Party just to simplify the situation. I had enough trouble just opening my locker and figuring out the best time to pop a zit. To make junk simple, you cut the complications. If the algebra gets too confusing, you don't admit that you're having troubles. That would just make you feel like the dunce with the funny hat in the corner. Instead of feeling that, you want to feel freedom so you just say forget this noise, chuck the paper in the trash. If the teacher don't like it, you give him the cupped hand. If you get suspended, grab the fishing pole and go to the Kalamazoo River. If that's too polluted, thumb a ride to Lake Michigan. If the fish is too big, you cut the bait. It's the same way with people. If your girlfriend talks too much, you give her the gag order. If she won't listen, you give her the gate. If the situation gets too complicated, you simplify the equation. That's how you find freedom.

"Forget that spade." That's what Donny Doortag told me. "He's just a dumb nigger."

"I'm tellin' you." And I wasn't just saying that. He was right, maybe could have been more original with the insults but we didn't think of that at the time. It was Michigan in the 70s. He was just calling a spade a spade. If you've never met a dumb nigger, you probably need to get out more often. Just like it's easy to hate people if you don't get to know them, it's a cinch to love them if you don't have to face them. That's why people love Pet Rocks and rock stars, Jimi Hendrix and dead people because it doesn't take a lick of sense or an ounce of courage to do that. You can be dumb as a whole box of Pet Rocks and get along with people you never meet. And most grownups weren't much help, had two ways of thinking. Some dismissed them all as a bunch of African jungle-bunnies. Others said stuff like color is only skin deep, we're all the same when it comes down to it. That didn't help because we knew black people were different, so if you were dim as a dunce and couldn't think for yourself, it was a cinch to go with the first viewpoint.

"They're all a bunch of dumb niggers."

"Uh-huh." I didn't say much when people like Donny said that because it was just like a guy calling all women bitches when he got mad at his girlfriend. You understood that because girls can be bitches. You knew that because girls ragged all the time, bitched about all boys just because they picked the wrong ones. If they would have picked me, they wouldn't have been so bitter and had all those problems. And those hassles didn't have anything to do with me, so they shouldn't have been putting me into that group. I didn't like that. That was just like calling black people niggers.

"That's just the way it is."

"Uh-huh." Donny was still talking about niggers. "Just forget about it."

"A nigger by any other name is still a nigger."

"Uh-huh." Usually I'd just say that, but if someone put my friends in that group, of course I spoke up. I'd known those kids for years, and they weren't complicating my situation, were actually helping me deal with stuff. I'd like to think I would have been open-minded about niggers no matter what, but who's to say what makes you the way you are or the way you ain't. It probably helped that my parents never said a word about this junk, just let us figure it out.

Of course, most adults were hell-bent on keeping us in our groups. This was that bizarre time in history when they'd make you check off boxes, constantly reminding you that you were going to be judged by the color of your skin. "Just check the box that says white."

"What?" That teacher must have been a prejudiced person, dumb as a box of crayons. Even though the other boxes used other words, it was all about colors, everybody knew that. "This don't seem right."

"It's to help people."

"How do it do that?" If somebody judges people by the shade of the skin or the color of the hair, that's called being prejudiced. If a teacher is that dumb, you can't even reason with her. I had learned junk by the time I was in junior high, but she was trying to send me back to kindergarten.

And actually in elementary, we judged people by their actions not by their colors. We were doing what Martin Luther King had said to do. His dream was me. Grownups got it all wrong.

"Did you complete the questionnaire?"

"You never gave me an answer. Why don't you do that? That's the problem."

"You do not need to get smart with me."

"Uh-huh." People think they get smarter when they get older, but actually they go backwards. She was just a dumb adult stuck in her ways, a dimwitted simpleton that didn't want to admit that to herself. She just wanted to make junk simple, shade all the kids into colors. "This is wrong."

"Just check the box." That teacher didn't have a clue, actually thought she was helping people get along or something. How can we get together when she's separating us into groups, telling us to pick a color and check off a box? That's like making colored people poop in different toilets.

"I gotta go to the bathroom."

"Did you fill out the form?"

"I gotta think about this before I do that." If we would have had stalls for the toilets, I could have gone and sat on the throne to ponder on this, but they didn't want us doing that.

"We need to move on with this."

"Okay, how about this, how come girls get stalls in their bathrooms? Tell me that."

"What does that have to do with filling out the form?"

"It's all part of a problem. It's society but you don't see that 'cause you're part of it."

"I think you need a referral."

"Go ahead and do that, but that don't change the facts." In fact, that's just more proof that she was a tool of society and she didn't even know that. And I'd just go to the head on the way to the office. "You can't gimme a referral just 'cause I gotta go to the john. That ain't right."

"If you want the bathroom pass, fill out the form. It's not that complicated."

"I ain't doin' it." In the future, I'd be judged for the junk I did. You couldn't just say my teacher made me do it. That ain't the way it works. Winches weren't regular people anyway, were just a bunch of American half-breeds, a mixed race of Slovakian peasants and Irish immigrants, didn't really fit in with normal people. Like one day, some kid came up to me.

"Hey, there's a white boy and a white girl sluggin' the crap out of each other."

"Big deal."

"Is that your brother and sister?"

"Who cares." But it was a little embarrassing for me, I have to admit that, to be different than everyone else. So it felt good to get along with the black girls. We'd played jump rope and hand games in elementary school, invented some new ones for junior high. "Gimme some skin."

"Slap five." Yvonne White would always give me a hand. "And don't gimme no jive."

"On the back side."

"Cuz you a bad boy." She'd slap the back of my hand. "A bad boy at the back of class."

"Yep." With a name like mine, you always found yourself there.

"Now poke that bad boy into my hole. Gimme the Winch worm."

"Okay." I'd wiggle my finger into her warm brown fist. "Give it a squeeze."

"You like it tight?"

"Yep." Moist too. "Moist like Duncan Hines."

"You got your finger in the birthday cake?"

"Fresh out the oven. And my favorite flavor."

"You get your finger through the chocolate frostin'?"

"Yep." I'd twist it around so I could rub her palm with the tip of my finger.

"Oh Winch. You gettin' good at this."

"I know." I could tell by the look on her face. "I think I can feel the creamy fillin'."

"What flavor is that?"

"I can't say till I taste it." But I'd heard it's pink as bubble-gum. "Maybe cherry."

"How do it feel?"

"It's tight."

"Don't choke on the cherry. Tight like what? Tight like I pumped up your birthday balloon too much?"

"So tight it might explode." Right in my pants. "Tight like hot pants."

"Skintight like your birthday suit's on too tight?"

"Tight like pushin' my big foot into your dinky sock."

"Tight like a rubber on Big Foot's you-know-what."

"Oh." That's a good one. "I bet it rhymes with sock."

"I bet you right. That too tight for you?"

"No, I liked that one."

"Tight like a tube-top on Dolly Parton."

"Oh yeah." I can picture that.

"Ain't you got a comeback? You had all night to think about this."

"I know." But I'd lose my thoughts once I pushed my finger in her hole.

"Tight like a gag on your big mouth."

"Tight like the knot that you got."

"Like the one I used to tongue-tie you?"

"Like the one on your sweatpants in PE."

"You took notice of that one?"

"Yep." I thought about that a lot.

"ARE YOU TWO IN BACK BEING RESPONSIBLE?"

"YEAH." I would have flipped that teacher the bird, but my finger was busy. "Where we at?"

"You were tryin' to get your hands in my sweatpants. I had you by the blue balls."

"Oh." That sounds like fun.

"Tight like your palm in my back pocket."

"That's more like it." I'd like to feel that.

"Tight like you're twistin' your small-appliance light bulb into my tight little socket."

"Tight like you're ridin' on my dirt bike. Like you're twistin' my throttle."

"Tight like a drunk clings to a bottle."

"Tight like your fist on my stick shifter."

"You switchin' gears on me. You goin' to auto shop on me. Just keep it tight."

"Okay." I'll try to do that. "Tight like your clamp on my battery post."

"I got it clamped on the positive side. You keep it grounded."

"Okay." Just don't stop squeezing it.

"Ain't you got nuh'un else in your tool belt?"

"Whaddya got in your toolbox?"

"If you wanna get your hands in there, you gotta know how to pick the lock."

"Okay." That's what I'm trying to do.

"I'll tell you what. It's just like you like it. It's tight like a nut on a bolt."

"I bet." It sure feels that way.

"Maybe it's time you loosen that nut and drain the forty-weight."

"I know." My pants were starting to feel tight. It was time to slip my other hand in my pocket and slide my thing behind my Playboy Bunny belt buckle. "Tight like a torque wrench."

"Tight like a fan belt."

"Tight like your connectin' rod clamped on my crankshaft."

"Gentlemen start your engines."

"Tight like a big-fat tire peelin' out on the blacktop."

"Now you rollin'. Burnin' up the rubber. Go on wit' your bad self. I can feel the friction."

"I know." I could feel it too. "It's your turn."

"It's tight like rubber on a rim."

"Like whitewall tires on a Cadillac car. What about that?"

"Like white on black?"

"Like me and you."

"Don't polish my rims if you ain't fuh'na take me for a ride."

"You the one rubbin' my finger."

"Am I rubbin' it the wrong way?"

"No." But I didn't want to have a wet daydream in my pants. "I didn't say that."

"That's all I'm sayin'."

"You can say anything."

"You the one wigglin' your thing all around."

"I can wiggle more than that."

"Yeah, I heard about you white boys."

"Oh yeah?" I wondered what she'd heard. "You heard right."

"You got that big O on your big mouth. So shut it up or whip it out."

"Okay." I think she was asking for something. "Whaddya want?"

"You need it spelled out for you?"

"Yep." I did need that, and I knew if she had to explain it, she wouldn't want others to hear it.

"I'm a bad girl. I'm just axin' for a lickin'. Y'know what I'm sayin'?"

"You want me to spank your booty?"

"That ain't the kinda lickin' I'm talkin' about. I was just playin' with that phrase. Sometimes you about bright as a small-appliance bulb. My little red light needs a little lickin'. That's all I'm sayin'. Shut your mouth or spread them lips and show me what you got."

"Oh." My boner was about to start squirting. "I got my finger in your hole."

"That the cue that you had enough?"

"Yep." That was that. "I'm in your hole."

"Cuz we got soul."

"I know." That's how we'd always end it. I'd pull out my finger and fold it into my fist, hold up my knuckles to show her that I had the soul power. She had that too.

When it comes down to it, that's probably the junk that brings people together, saying let's forget our differences so we can get down to business. It ain't that complicated. Even if you don't want to change, girls can change your mind. Even if I was just pushing my finger into her fist, that felt like the start of something. In the beginning, it was just the *slap five, back side, in the hole, we got soul,* but once I got my finger in there, I'd try to think of anything to make it last.

That girl wanted something from me but I didn't understand what it was, what I could have that black boys didn't. I took showers with them, didn't see anything missing. I was more than ready to give her what she wanted, but she had to point me in the right direction. If she wanted me to lick her little red light, she'd have to tell me where she kept it. I'd already made some mistakes that year, didn't want to feel dense like that again. Females should come with instructions.

Of course, I certainly understood them black chicks more than the other girls, used to laugh out loud with them in the middle of class, when the teacher and other kids didn't seem to understand what's so funny in the first place. Even when you couldn't explain it, it was good to have people you could relate with, especially if they were females with butts and boobs.

I know for a fact that Nannette Culpepper was always nice to me, tickling my ribs and cheesing at me in the morning, sometimes sneaking up behind me and putting her soft brown hands over my eyeballs, whispering *Guess who?* in my ear. I will never forget that, still dig that girl for doing that. She had her hair all bunched up in marbles and braids, was just a short little seventh-grader but I wasn't any taller.

One time, me and Nannette were in Home Ec, sitting at our Singer Genie with her helping me stitch up that apron we had to make, and she told me that I was the only white boy in that whole dumb school that was nice to her. That made me sad and happy at the same time, made me think about the reason because she was sweeter than that pound cake we got to make, to me at least. Now that I think about it, I should have made her my girlfriend, maybe offered her a St. Christopher necklace, at least asked her if she wanted that. I just didn't have the guts, barely even considered it. It was just out of the question. A white boy might say he wanted to get some from a black girl, but few even said that, and nobody talked about anything to do with how I felt about Nannette.

Of course, that helped make it innocent and low stress, simple like friendship, not sweating about all that other junk. When it came down to it, I wasn't even sure I knew how to do that stuff.

But still I liked looking when they walked and wiggled away, foxy chocolate-covered females like Veronica Poplar and Gloria Stafford, me leaning against the railing in the hallway and nudging Mike Wilson in the ribs, wishing I had the balls he had. He was black as a freshly paved two-lane but he had himself a real-live white chick for a girlfriend. She was a big-mouthed girl with jet-black hair but her skin was pale as those lines in the road. Of course, she might as well have been black, certainly talked like she was, got in fist-fights like the black girls did, was always yelling at Mike.

She was nice to me for the most part but mostly just wanted me to keep an eye on Mike, would even pull me aside and tell me that, that she trusted me to do just that. When me and Mike were hanging out, he never let her tag along, and maybe she had reasons to rag because Mike didn't let all that nagging stop him from two-timing, or at least trying, flirting and making a fool of himself.

Actually, he never really dogged on her, just liked practicing his rap with the black chicks. The main goal of rapping was to get some necking or nookie action but it was more than that, usually just a way to get some jollies. The black guys had it down, made rapping into an art form.

I used to cop a lean on the rapping rail, listen to Wilson and Terry Buchanan and all them black kids making bets, pocketing the chump change if they could get a grin from a girl. It was a freestyle competition without a doubt, but this was 1975 and they didn't call it that, just mimicked Muhammad Ali and people like that, mostly avoided the rhyming because that was kind of corny, double-dutch stuff for the girls on the playground. At Hillside, it was all about rapping to chicks and getting the grin, echoism about getting some, almost-rhyming and getting some jollies, slapping skin and smelling fingers. And of course, a black girl would usually spin around like a boomerang, everybody getting all crazy. I'd just sit and grin, listen and laugh, thought that was a crack up, but if I could redo anything, I'd go back in time and give it a try, go right up and French-kiss Veronica Poplar right on the lips. Even if she slugged me for doing that, I'd still say it was worth it.

Of course, at the time I didn't have all the answers, and having a black girlfriend was certainly out of the question, so when it came to females, I mostly hung out with the stoner girls, cute chicks like Debbie Hurley and Jackie Joseph, pinching their butts and scribbling weed leaves on their blue jeans, band logos on their denim-covered school binders, hugs in the hallway, smokes after school. I didn't know much, but I knew how to hug a girl and French-inhale a Newport, went professional as an artist, used to do drawings that other kids would use to impress some lady, fibbing to the interest about who did it. If you slipped me a couple quarters, I was glad to help out.

If my classmates asked, I would slide them the answers, knew how they felt, just like me, liked getting in trouble because it was one thing we were good at, chucking paper wads when Mr. Burch wasn't looking, sharing Newports in the woods before school started, skipping class whenever we felt like it. I was never a rebel, far from it, just seeking attention, trying to fit in and hoping to catch the consideration of some female. If your boyfriend was too much of a wuss, you could ask Winch and he'd take you, grab your hand and hitchhike to the indoor shopping mall. I'd use my milk money or artist earnings to buy you a soft pretzel, sit by the fountain with our butts touching, flick a nickel and make a wish, rogue you a weed-leaf belt buckle, maybe some turquoise Thunderbird earrings from the booth in the hall, no doubt about that. I didn't know how to say no when it came to females, was a fool for any fur or fox, even a skinny girl as long as she had something to squeeze and nobody was looking, or even a chubby semi-ugly one if she had that sparkle in her eyes, I never said no to any of them, or to skipping school or swiping junk, smoking a bowl or whatever.

Of course I'm just bragging, keeping it vague to make it sound like I was getting some. The truth of the matter, I didn't have a clue when it came to the girl stuff, was thrilled just to nibble on some pretty girl's ABC chewing gum, happy if I could get close enough to sniff that Jolly Rancher smell in her ponytail. I was in heaven if I could hold her hand, maybe even taste the Orange Crush Lip Smacker on her tongue but that was about it. Once you got to the peach fuzz, I had heard you were supposed to eat it but that didn't seem right, knew to cop a feel but that girl at the drive-in told me not to squeeze so hard, *THAT HURTS*, tell me something else, I need some instruction.

It ain't like later when kids on the computers would get close-up lessons, maybe not good ones but something to go on, and meanwhile, we were on our own, but I know that was the beginning of that idea of never saying no to nothing. I had enough regrets anyway, wished I'd made the moves on Laura Rushmore after the school dance that night, what was I thinking, never should have let go of Lindsey Bowman's hand that skate-date Saturday at Oshtemo Roller Rink, and while I'd never really get that girl junk down, I had other stuff figured out. You don't think about it, just go for it, and Debbie Hurley was always game, we were two of a kind, went together like bud in a bowl, doing baseball-bat no-smoke tokers in the back of the library, spraying the Ozium and chewing on Quench gum, meeting at the Little League field after school, sometimes staying up all night.

That girl made me feel mellow, like nicotine after getting high in the woods in the morning. She calmed my nerves, used to rub my bellybutton with her finger. I didn't know why she did that, but it made me giggle and feel better. I remember her like smoking cigarettes, always skipped out of typing class, meeting her in the hall and off to the girls' bathroom, hiding in the stall and puffing on her Kools, me sitting on the back of the toilet so my feet wouldn't show. That was great, especially that one time Jolly Molly Falvey came in and pinched a loaf. When she was washing her hands, I couldn't stop myself, had to walk out. She was such a cool chick, I don't know why I did that.

Another time, I was sitting in typing class with my fingers on the home-row position and all of a sudden, in ran Debbie Hurley, a gang of grownups chasing her down, the fuzz and her probation officer, principals Rag and Armstrong, knocking over desks and typewriters, manuals and electric Olivettis crashing to the floor, and when Debbie got behind me with her hands on my shoulders, I knew to stand up and get set for a serious fight. I put up my dukes, was ready for anything.

But luckily Argo was a cool teacher, taught typing and coached JV football and wrestling, and he liked Debbie, likely unlike most teachers, and he got everyone cooled out and calmed down. They probably took her back to juvie, but I'd stood up and that made all the difference, to me at least.

Debbie maybe always took things a bit too far, but I understood that, wanted to stomp my irregular sneakers at the edge of everything, wanted to do anything that could be done, knew there was more to life than flicking boogers out the bus window and sitting in the back of science class, and if it killed me, so be it, I didn't care, I just didn't want to miss one second of the fun, and Debbie was someone that seemed to be with me on that. I still love that girl for being like that.

Of course, she was a girl and Jackie was her best friend. I had a crush on Jackie but I wasn't good with girls when they were my friends, could kiss strangers at the drive-in right on the lips, but if I knew them too well, I felt stupid trying to do that. I had my friends, black guys like Mike Wilson, stoner chicks and other fry-brains, lots of them probably but I didn't have a best friend that wasn't tied down with a girlfriend. Mike was game with most everything but he had his woman, and he was black, said being a black man is dangerous enough, didn't see no reason to get all stupid. Besides, it's hard to get away with junk when you're always getting noticed, when you stood out like a broken egg on a black Cadillac by his house, or like an afro on a snowman in my block. That didn't matter to me and Mike, at least when it was just a half-dozen people, but when it was more like a hundred, that was a different story. "I'm the only black person here."

"Is that how you feel?"

"It ain't really about the way I feel."

"What is it?"

"It's just the way it is." That's what he told me, but I didn't understand what he was saying until it was the other way around. Still, we didn't think much about it, just knew that other people were taking notice. That's no way to start a crime wave, not the best situation for that. Maybe I still talked with Rick Poling, but he'd transferred to Catholic school and I was a different person, liked what I was doing, running down something, twelve years old, headed to thirteen with a vengeance, and I needed an accomplice, a friend who was game for anything and everything, and one winter day, I was walking home from wrestling, the day after they took our team picture and I'd gotten away with that obscene gesture, and me and Louie Palladino were walking along and started talking, both had big families, didn't get a ride home, had a few miles of hoofing. I don't remember what we talked about, but we talked, and after that evening, we became the best of friends, something more important than everything else in the world combined, plus even more than that.

PUMP ACTION

Right off the bat, me and Louie saw things the same way, and we both knew that to have some fun we'd need some firearms, at the very least a pellet gun, thumbed through the Monkey Wards catalog and looked at the underwear girls, picked out the rifle, saved up to get it.

Once we scored it, we were out of control, shooting out every window we could find, every bird in the neighborhood had better watch out. It was a Crossman pump-action pellet gun with a scope, and we'd pump it up twenty times, until you could barely snap that piece of plastic back home.

Pretty soon we had battles with anybody with a bb gun, put football helmets on our heads and hoped for the best, tried not to aim for the eyeballs. Sure, some stuck and they all stung, left marks that itched at night, but that's just the way it goes, the price you pay for having tons of fun.

Of course most of the time, it was just me and Louie, roaming the neighborhood like natives in the jungle, looking for prey. One afternoon, Louie actually nailed a bird, dropped a sparrow from a branch, snapped its spine at the base of the neck. When I held that tiny bird in my hand, rolled its head around, that didn't make us feel good. I set it down on the grass and tried to move on.

We learned our lesson, that's what happened, stopped shooting birds, moved on to pigeons. We'd pump up the Crossman five or ten times and plug them in the side, give them a good scare. They'd circle around and land the same place, wait to get thumped again. Pretty soon, it was no fun, like picking on a cripple, or a dimwitted kid or something like that. We weren't evil.

But plugging kids was always a blast, crawling on Louie's roof and waiting for them to pedal by on their banana seats sporting tank tops, windbreakers or whatever, it didn't matter, they were easy targets. When you'd squeeze the trigger, they didn't know what hit them, thought they got stung by a wasp or something, that was great, nailing cars, aiming for hubcaps, ringing the bell, that's what we did, every day after school. But one time, the lady in the back seat spotted me.

"She sees you."

"Yep." She sure did.

"You still gonna shoot it?"

"Course." I shook my bangs, lined up the cross hairs on her forehead, took aim at the face looking out the window. In fact, she was the bride, riding in the limo, on the way to her wedding. I squeezed the trigger, watched the window explode, listened to the whitewalls screech to a stop.

"LET'S BOOK!"

"I'm hip." We flew through the attic window, raced through the house, booked out the back door, but of course we were busted from the get-go. Louie's big sister was home, and she was none too happy, decided it was better if the folks didn't know, held that mistake over our heads for a few years, made us pay for the window. But we had no regrets, it's just like the ooh and the ouch from getting hit in the face with a pellet, the price you pay for getting your kicks.

After that we maybe lost the right to bear arms, but we didn't care, had had our fun, guns were for hunters and hillbillies anyway, we were city rats and at that time, weapons were for wussies. And besides, we always had wrist-rockets and bottle-rockets, Roman candles, drop a cherry bomb in a tennis-ball can and you had yourself a grenade launcher. We burned most everything we had, filled our models with gasoline and firecrackers, lit them on fire, watched them explode and melt down to globs of plastic, torched all the toys from our past and hightailed into the future.

RUM & SNEAKERS

Streaking was something people had done for years. It was a fad, stripping down to your sneakers and tube socks and running around naked. But that was before my time. I'd never done it. And I'd never gotten drunk, but that was all about to change. It was 1976, the summer between seventh and eighth grade. Me and Louie had a fifth of rum and his parents were gone. We stood in his backyard and downed that bottle, chugged it so fast we weren't even drunk when we drained it.

"You drunk?"

"Nope." Louie shook his mop-top. "I don't think."

"Me neither."

"I don't feel nothin'."

"I'm hip."

"Maybe we just have to wait."

"Maybe you're right."

"I hope."

"Same here." After a while, Louie started taking off his cut-offs. "Whaddya doin'?"

"I don't feel like wearin' pants no more."

"I'm hip." I took off mine. "Forget pants, man."

"I know." He dropped his JCPennys, kicked them into the bushes. "Forget underwear too."

"Forget that noise."

"For days." Pretty soon, we'd stripped down to our sneakers. "That feels better."

"Tons."

"I think I'm drunk now."

"I think you are."

"Are you?"

"Yep." I grabbed my balls. "I'm pretty sure I am."

"Whaddya wanna do?"

"Let's go bust some junk."

"No doubt." So that's what we did, ran around getting rowdy. By Henderson Park, we ran into Mark Pulaski. "HEY PULASKI."

"What's the deal?"

"We're drunk."

"As a skunk."

"Where's your pants?"

"Who cares." I climbed the lamppost and busted the glass with my fist.

"WINCH!"

"WHAT?"

"That ain't cool."

"Oh." I was wasted, but knew Pulaski was right. "Big deal."

"C'mon." He was worried about us, which I thought was cool but it wasn't a reason to stop. We'd found our place in the world, out in the streets raising hell, and Louie was laughing and my fist was bleeding and we howled down Henderson Drive, butt-naked like newborn babies.

MAD DOG & TUBE-TOPS

After the rum, we mostly stuck to beer and wine, whatever we could rogue from the store. Sure, we'd grab the hard stuff if we could get that, but that was behind the counter, harder to get, and we'd usually end up puking out our guts, waking up with the pillow pasted to my cheek, or even worse, waking up outside with my face stuck to the sidewalk, that was the worst, so we'd usually take it easy so we wouldn't get too drunk, just chug-a-lug eight-packs of Little Kings, cases of Miller High Life, the champagne of beers, wash it down with a bottle of Mad Dog. At first, we'd grab the wrong kinds of wine, ones with corks, but we'd drink that anyway, push down the corks with the butt of my jackknife. Once we even swiped vanilla flavoring because we read the label, knew it had alcohol. Of course that didn't work, and over time we learned what to snab, stuck with the beer, and the wines with the screw-off caps because those were the best, Boone's Farm and Mad Dog, Annie Green Springs if you had some fur to share it with. Chicks loved that junk.

We'd always walk Harley to his games at the Little League field, stop at Avenue Party Store and rogue a bottle of MD 20/20, hoof to the baseball diamonds and swipe some Bubble Yum and Bottle Cap candy from the concession stand, flirt with the pretty girls leaning against the wall, pull at their Levi tags and yank at their pockets sticking out the bottoms of their cut-offs, try to rogue a kiss and get nothing, forget about them and go get drunk with the tube-topped chubby girls in the bushes. We'd drain the wine before we got there, but the tube-top twins would always have rum, pour the 151 over the tops of their cherry sno-cones, let you suck the color from their shaved ice.

That rum-and-cherry molasses was one of my favorite flavors, stuck to my tongue like a good memory, that was fun as anything, getting drunk and talking naughty, rolling around on the ground with those girls, reading tags and laughing, snapping elastic, licking cherry from their bellybuttons and getting all sticky and dirty, getting down to the real nitty-gritty. Of course once we got there, we didn't know what to do with it, didn't have a clue even when we knocked all our heads together.

Me and Louie realized that we had no reason to get tied down with some females anyway, that's what we decided, left them there in the bushes. They were laughing about something, had obviously gotten their jollies and we had our hickies, forming like memories. With Louie, I'd finally found someone who was game for anything and we didn't need some chicks keeping us down.

"If they don't wanna know the deal, that's their loss."

"That's a fact." And other guys were even worse, like little girls when it came to breaking the law and having fun, had to go home because their mommies were calling, had to go change their tampons or something, always had some stupid reason why we shouldn't do this or that. Harley was with us some of the time, but he worried too much, needed some coaxing. Like one day, we were walking him to Little League, listening to him bitch about how he never gets on the mound.

"I always get stuck in the outfield."

"That sucks."

"Big donkey dicks."

"Might as well get drunk."

"Gimme that bottle."

"Now you're talkin'."

"I never get to pitch anyway."

"Chug it all."

"Awright." So that's what he did. When we got to the game, me and Louie copped a lean on the bleachers. We knew this was going to be good.

"HARLEY," the coach yelled. "YOU'RE ON THE MOUND TODAY."

"I get to pitch?"

"This is your chance."

"Oh." We could see Harley wasn't sure about this.

"Show me what you got."

"Okay."

"You awright?"

"Yeah." That's what Harley said, but we knew he was headed for trouble. When he started chucking the ball over the backstop, nobody thought that was funny, except me and Louie, busting our guts, falling off the bleachers. Harley upchucked, tried to catch the purple puke in his mitt, but that didn't work. Finally he knew he had nothing left to lose, started laughing along with us.

That was the day Harley graduated from Little League, made it to the big leagues, joined me and Louie getting drunk in the bushes. That's where the action is anyway.

HOMEGROWN FREEDOM

That summer, it was the year of America's 200th birthday, everything printed or painted red, white and blue, cans of beer and buildings downtown, banners across the streets, Bicentennial flags on the poles, the Freedom Train stopping at the Amtrak station. Of course, we didn't give a rat's ass about all that, had other plans, found our own way to celebrate the birthday. We'd heard about this guy that had a garden of pot plants growing in his backyard, figured it was meant to be, time to start toking tons of herb, as long as it was free. It was supposed to be a free country anyway.

This one chubby kid had told us about it, was hoping we'd let him into the gang if he shared this knowledge. His plan was to just grab one plant each, leave the rest behind so the guy wouldn't get too ticked off. He wanted to make sure we were clear on this, that this was his plan so he should be able to make the rules of the rip-off. We just nodded and agreed to his nonsense. We didn't say anything to each other, but it was the era of excess, double-live albums, long guitar solos, no reason for restraint. As soon as I found myself in a jungle of pot plants, the excitement of it all just went to my head. I started snabbing anything I could get, uprooting every stalk I could hold.

I guess I was making a lot of noise, pretty excited about finding free weed. The guy came out the back door with a baseball bat, looking pretty pissed off. I knew he wasn't about to call the fuzz, but it looked like he had other plans, his days of peace and understanding had come to an end.

Of course I wasn't too worried, had run cross-country and track-and-field that year at school, knew nobody could outrun a Winch. I grabbed a few more stalks till I had half of his crop under my arms, just ducked and swung the branches in his face, took off along the fences behind the houses, out to Grand Avenue, running down the middle of the street in the middle of the day, dirt shaking from the roots, the mass of weed leaves dragging behind me.

When we got to Louie's backyard, that chubby kid was all pissed off, but me and Louie told him to quit the bitching, were happy we'd gotten away with all that weed and hardly a scratch, just a few on our legs, who cares about that. "That's a small price to pay for what we got."

"I'm hip." We didn't see no reason to be upset about nothing. The sun was shining and we had a bunch of free weed.

"Okay, let's split it up." That other kid thought he was entitled to a third of the booty because he was the one who had discovered the pickings in the first place. "That's only fair."

"Forget that noise." He just wanted to grab one, and that's what he did, so take your one plant and get out of here, get dick and screw you too. He didn't even smoke weed anyway.

So we said later to him, and we were set that summer, dried the plants on the picnic table in Louie's backyard because parents didn't know squat about pot back then, we just made up some story about something, dried out the pot plants and got a pack of Zig Zag papers, rolled up some fat joints, fired them up and got good and toasted, smoked some more just for the heck of it.

Homegrown was okay with us, swimming at the swimming pool was tons more fun, like it had been the first time we did that, getting our jollies, sneaking into the Elks Club and going off the high dive, eyeballing the rich fur girls in the candy-striped bikinis, the lifeguard blowing her whistle, *NONE OF THAT*, kicking us out. We'd smoke more weed and hoof over to West Main Mall, flipping out at Spencer Gifts, laughing at the toilet jokes and gag gifts, tripping at the plastic flowers with the laser-light fibers, black-light posters, free greaze on toothpicks at Hickory Farms, smoking more mean-green and sneaking into a movie, splitting if it wasn't action packed, staying for the blood and guts, the boobs and the laughs, toking weed right in the theater, back when smoking was allowed while you watched a movie, *The Bad News Bears* and *The Gauntlet, Jaws* and *Carrie* and *Car Wash,* the Detroit man on *Moving Violation, The Cassandra Crossing* and Led Zeppelin's *The Song Remains the Same*, junk like that. That was a blast.

"That's a fact."

"What's next?"

"Good question."

"Let's shake up some action."

"I'm hip." That summer belonged to us and nobody else. We did give a rat's ass if it was right or wrong, we knew what we had, and we were grabbing it with both hands.

"Check that MG Midget."

"I'm on it." If someone left the keys in his ignition, we'd go for a joyride, go get our jollies, swiping hood ornaments by the bag full, just for the heck of it, shouting *STARSKY AND HUTCH* and running over the top of a car, jumping from the hood to the trunk of another, stuffing 12-packs in the canvas bag left over from my *Detroit Free Press* paper route and running down the street, out every night doing whatever we could find, busting streetlights and torching yard signs, smoking bowls and giving shotguns, sleeping in and heading out when people went to work, breaking into houses in the broad daylight, swiping junk and heading to the next adventure.

FRISKY IN FRISCO

Near the middle of July, I took a plane to see my dad in California. He usually took the family on a trip, but that summer he went by himself. Maybe I should have known the reasons he did that, but I was just glad to take a vacation. It was the only time I took a trip with just my dad.

I met him in San Francisco, and we stayed with some college students. I didn't really know what to do, mostly just mumbled back then and usually nobody understood me so I thumbed through the records, and one of the good-looking chicks living there told me to pick something.

"Okay." I spotted a cover I'd seen in Harley's collection, thought Harley was a dipshit when it came to music, never listened to that crap but I recognized one album, picked that one out.

"Wow." She took the gatefold. "I'm impressed."

"Uh-huh." I knew the deal.

"That's great." The whole time we were there, she always played that album, looking at me and nodding, me smiling and nodding back, trying not to puke. It was the worst music I'd ever heard. "If you like George Benson, you'll love this."

"Great." I can't wait.

"You ready to go?"

"Yep." My dad always saved me, got me out of there. They'd just invented the rule that you needed a credit card to rent a car so we didn't have any wheels, hitchhiked to the beach, got picked up by this guy with an old Malibu Classic and a huge bag of Colombian gold.

"You guys smoke pot?"

"No." That's what my dad said. When we got out, he told me about guys like that, pitiful lonely people like that guy with his big bag of marijuana. I didn't feel too bad for him.

We went to the beach but I don't really remember that, just remember the ride back. We got picked up by a Dodge van, the weed smoke rolling out when this chick pulled open the side door. Her skin was tanned and her hair was smooth, parted in the middle, bleached by the sunshine. She was the best-looking girl I'd ever seen in my whole life, sporting a lime-green bikini bottom and an airbrushed tank top, the weed leaf faded, the fabric like thermal underwear, no bra.

"Jump in."

"Thanks." Some fry-brain was driving, some ugly old pothead that was way too old for that chick. My dad sat in the shotgun seat and I got to ride in the back, sitting on a bed with that girl. There was a curtain so my dad and the driver couldn't see us. "Is that your boyfriend?"

"Nope." She put her arm around me. "I'm free."

"Cool." I could have died right then and there, could have spent the rest of my life in the back of that van. And I finally learned why my older brothers had loved living out West.

"You wanna smoke some weed?"

"No." Let's do something else.

"You're frisky."

"Yep." I figured these were my fifteen minutes of fame, didn't want to waste one second.

"YOU OKAY BACK THERE?"

"Uh-huh." I could tell my dad wasn't too comfortable with the situation, but the guy driving seemed okay with it, kept talking to my dad, giving me time to get to know that girl. She had a crease in her bikini and a smile on her face that was warm as the weather. When we got back to the house, I still had a big boner and the college lady wanted to turn me on to some more music.

"Wait till you hear this."

"I've got to go to the bathroom."

"When you've got to go, you've got to go."

"Yep." That's true. After I got done in there and I was done with my vacation, that lady gave me a ride to the airport. I'd already learned that California girls will make the moves on you. I was waiting for her to do that, but she just talked about modern jazz and played her crappy cassettes.

"It was fun listening to music with you."

"Uh-huh." I got to sit next to this other foxy college lady on the airplane, kept taking her cigarettes when she'd offer them. I was trying to be cool, figured maybe she'd take me back to her pad, front me some more Merits after she had her way with me. She probably had a waterbed.

"You okay?"

"Yeah." But I was feeling dizzy from puffing too much.

"You sure?"

"Yep." I thought I'd make it, but we had to circle the airport. I puked in the magazine pouch, hoping that foxy lady didn't notice. But I think she did. I know she didn't take me home, and I never got to find out if she had a waterbed. But I still think she did, thought about that a lot.

After I was done thinking about that, I got on the phone. "What's the deal?"

"How was California?"

"Cool." I told Louie about the foxy girl with the sun-bleached hair and weed-leaf tank top. And that crease in her bikini. "She was a fur and a half."

"You mauled with her?"

"And then some." And I respected her as a person.

"You copped a feel?"

"For days." And I remembered not to squeeze it too hard. "It felt good."

"Did you get her telephone number?"

"Yep." And her address.

"Did she write it?"

"Nuh'un but." I got it right here.

"You gotta get over here so I can see it. And give you some skin."

"You got some of that homegrown left?"

"Tons."

"In a minute." Louie lived around the corner, about fifteen houses away if you went the long way, but my backyard was big, nearly stretched back to Buckley Street. I just stomped the fence, jumped down to Mr. Buckley's back lot, b-lined across that and busted through the bushes to Louie's backyard, didn't even have to knock on the door, just walked right in, snabbed a pop from the frig and booked up the stairs, knocked on Louie's headphones. "What's the deal?"

"JAMMIN' OUT."

"Zeppelin?"

"What else."

"Like a mug."

126

"Gimme five."

"Ten."

"I'm hip."

"Put on some pants."

"Just a sec."

"You got any brew?"

"Course." It was a hot summer day and he was all ready for my return. "At the shed."

"Let's go." The space between our houses belonged to Mr. Buckley, but he was older than that Oldsmobile stored in his garage, even older than that Edsel next to it, probably born in the last century, grew up before wheels were even invented. The shed was attached to the back of his garage and we had made that our own, had the walls decorated with the side emblems we'd rogued from rides. We had that technique down, just slid a butter knife behind them, popped them off, clipped the hood ornaments with wire-cutters, had a good collection going.

But our favorite spot was the roof of the shed so I put the wrist-rocket in my back pocket and gave Louie a boost, climbed up there and copped a lean against the back of the garage. Louie reached into the open window and propped open the cooler, grabbed two bottles. "Still got your opener?"

"Yep." Still got my fang tooth. "Last time I checked."

"Ready to chug?"

"I was born ready."

"I'm hip." We held out the bottles. "One tip."

"And nuh'un but."

"Cuz you ain't lame."

"And you ain't no lightweight."

"Here's to us."

"All for one and all for us."

"I'll drink to that." And that's what we did, chugged the beers and flicked the empties on the ground, shot them with our wrist-rockets and grabbed the next round. The yard was all overgrown with weeds and trees growing up through the cracks in the basketball court, vines taking claim on the pole, the whole lot bordered with so many trees so nobody could see us. And the attic of the garage had plenty of room to stash anything we had, like those Hefty bags full of homegrown.

"There's tons left."

"Pounds."

"At the minimum."

"To the max."

"Pack up a bowl."

"I'm on it." He grabbed the Nixon bong from the window, dumped out the water and filled it with beer, packed the bowl with the homegrown. "So your old man was right in the van?"

"No doubt."

"What's your dad doin' out in California anyway?"

"Beats me." Maybe I should have known that my parents were headed for a divorce or at least that my dad was out there looking for my brother. "He's just takin' a vacation."

"Did you bring the phone number?"

"Yep." I pulled it from my wallet. "That's it."

"That's good handwritin'."

"I'm hip." The best.

"I can tell she's a fur."

"And a half."

"Maybe she's got a sister."

"You wish."

"I hope." He lit the bowl, handed it to me. "So California was cool?"

"Yep." It was. "But it's good to be back."

"Good to have you back, man."

"Yep." I hit the carb and grabbed his hand, just smoking mean-green and downing beers, talking trash and shooting bottles but that day was hot and humid and that beer was good and cold, the best-tasting suds in the whole wide world. We sat on that roof until the sun went down.

Louie graduated from Michigan State University, moved to sunny California and met a beautiful girl. He settled in the Bay Area with his wife and children.

Winch graduated from Hillside Junior High.

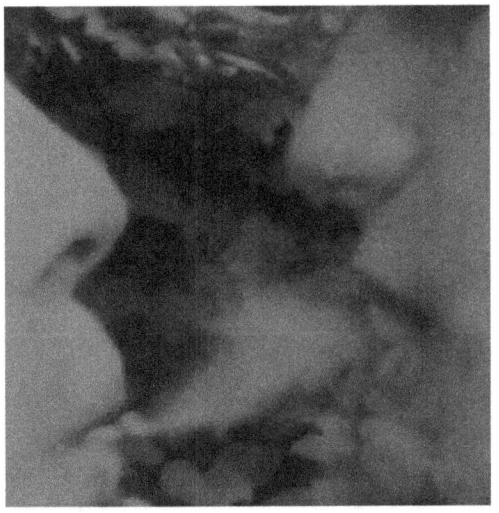

Me and Louie 1979
  (shotgun at the rope swing)
  photo by Dave Middleton

Winch
Lake Michigan (21st Century)

Winch
California (21st Century)

Winch currently lives in Wichita, Oregon. He writes music reviews and a travel blog at eight-track.com.

Other titles by Winch
Motor City Jailbait: Junk Like That (Book One)
Motor City Junior High: Junk Like That (Book Two)

Please post comments or review of this book at Amazon
Or email comments to winchmartin@live.com

Eight Track Publishing
9408 SE Hollywood Avenue
Milwaukie, OR 97222

eight-track.com

www.ingramcontent.com/pod-product-compliance
Lightning Source LLC
Chambersburg PA
CBHW070337130626
46556CB00007B/2908